The author was born on the Isle of Wight, making him a true caulkhead. His childhood was full of adventures. A lot of the coastline he played along as a child hasn't changed and still gives him great inspiration for his books, as he can sit on the same pieces of old stonewall or climb the worn-out steps like the character in his book does, the same way he did all those years ago as a child.

Dedicated, with love, to my wife, Claire. This book would have not been possible without her love and support.

Leabo Jangles

CASTLE COVE:
THE NEW SORCERESS

AUSTIN MACAULEY PUBLISHERS™

LONDON • CAMBRIDGE • NEW YORK • SHARJAH

A CIP catalogue record for this title is available from the British Library.

ISBN 9781528901918 (Paperback)
ISBN 9781528901925 (Hardback)
ISBN 9781528957212 (ePub e-book)

www.austinmacauley.com

First Published (2020)
Austin Macauley Publishers Ltd
25 Canada Square
Canary Wharf
London
E14 5LQ

I would like to thank everyone at Austin Macauley for their belief in me and my book.

Chapter 1

Professor Billingham quickly made his way down a hallway which was poorly lit by flickering lamps. His long, drawn-out coat was warm and shabby, flowing out behind him as he carried his tatty briefcase by his side.

Reaching the library door, he tapped it twice with haste, turning the sea serpent doorknob.

"Professor, I am so glad you managed to get here so quickly," said Mr Wolverton, his voice quivering as he held out a hand with anticipation to greet his dear old friend. The Professor looked over the top of his bifocals with a serious gaze.

"Your telephone message sounded urgent. I take it that is still the case?" said Professor Billingham, sounding out of breath as he reached for a chair nearby.

A very eccentric Mr Wolverton turned and walked over to the corner of his library to an orderly stack of charts.

"I'm afraid so," Mr Wolverton said as he knelt down, moving the charts to one side, revealing a very old chest, carved with strange markings. The chest was held together by thick, sturdy metal straps nailed down solid. Grasping one of the handles carefully, he pulled it out from its hiding place. Mr Wolverton was forced to drag it across the floor, struggling as he lifted the chest up onto the table. Walking to another part of the room, he looked amongst countless books upon shelves, stacked from floor to ceiling. Many were of great importance. As the light changed, the books appeared in many shapes and sizes of great proportion telling stories of outer space and the mysteries of the deep sea.

Climbing up the steps, Mr Wolverton slid around on the step rail, holding on he reached out balancing himself pulling one from the shelves. His heart was racing as he turned the blank front cover only to discover inside, a key cut into the pages which was long and appeared rusty with age. Removing it, he replaced the book and carefully stepped down making his way back over to the table. Looking at the Professor who gave him a nod with an uneasy, troubled expression, he pushed the key into the lock halfway before a complex sequence of levers clicked and moved into place. There was a rotation mechanism as he pulled the key free, lifting the lid.

In that moment, an intense blaze of light filled the room, so dazzling that both men looked away until their eyes had adjusted. Slowly, they leaned forward, peering in. What they witnessed together at that moment they had watched countless times before; however, each time they were amazed at its beauty for there in front of them lay a glass orb. The orb hovered in the middle of the chest filled with a light so great, as it turned into a mass of flaming orange fire. It appeared so strong that the glow made the two men turn away after just a few moments.

Professor Billingham reached deep into his shabby briefcase, pulling out a pair of goggles with thick, dark lenses that withstood extreme light. Once he had positioned them protecting his eyes, he leaned forward and peered back into the chest. All the time Mr Wolverton paced the room, arms crossed, trying not to fear the worst. It was five minutes more before the Professor looked up, took off his goggles and reached into his shirt pocket pulling out his hanky. Wiping the sweat from his brow, he appeared as though the sun had gazed upon him too long, red-faced leaving two white circles where his goggles had been. Stuffing his hanky back into his pocket, he looked at his friend who was eagerly waiting for an answer.

"Well, I am certain there is something; it is very hard to make sense of it at the moment. I'm not sure if it means anything or not," said Professor Billingham.

"Yes, Professor, but it's never changed before; it has always stayed the same showing us both orange and yellow fire. There has never been a shadow of darkness captured in the middle," questioned Mr Wolverton.

"I understand what you're saying. Normally, I would be the first to agree with you, but this could have happened before without anyone realising. You, your father, and even your grandfather may not have noticed it. It may not have shown itself to you."

"But it worries me, Professor. The darkness in the orb, even if it is tiny, something may be happening on the other side. I'm sure of it," said Mr Wolverton.

The Professor closed the lid firmly on the chest; the light gradually disappeared as he turned to face his friend.

"If you are certain, you must prepare Ashlee as they may need her quicker than first thought. You must be ready to send her through," said Professor Billingham.

Mr Wolverton with strain in his face and holding his head in his hands said, "I have feared this day all my life. Deep down I wished it would have skipped my generation, hoping it would never happen." The Professor paced up and down the room rubbing his chin.

"If your fears are right, then we are entering an unknown time and no amount of reading will help prepare Ashlee for what could happen. In the meantime, I will phone the university and take urgent leave. Then I can be close by if something does happen."

"Thank you, Professor. I feel much happier having you nearby," sighed Mr Wolverton as he placed his hand upon his friend's shoulder.

"From tomorrow, I will take Ashlee down to the beach in preparation for the opening of the door. Maybe we should break the news to Mrs Rose."

Chapter 2

Sabella and Ashlee finished their first meal of the day. Breakfast consisted of eggy bread with freshly squeezed orange juice which was Sabella's favourite and a family tradition. As they both got down from the table, Mrs Rose turned around from the kitchen sink wearing her apron. Always wearing gloves to protect her overlong fingernails, she was a tall lady with long wispy grey hair, pale skin and her blue eyes sparkled. Mrs Rose had a love for flowery dresses, whatever the occasion and felt happiest at home in the kitchen. To her it was the hub of the home where everyone came to eat, talk and be a family. There was nothing more she loved than spending her days baking and coming up with new recipes. The wonderful smell would waft through the house of fresh bread and cakes, her speciality being a fine Victoria sponge cake, homemade jam and that all important secret ingredient.

"Now, listen, girls, you're not to go too far as Mr Wolverton has asked us to spend time at the beach today for a picnic. So, only as far as the garden please," said Mrs Rose as she began putting together the hamper.

As Ashlee skipped her way down through the house, she called Bosen, the basenji who jumped from his bed and scampered down the hallway narrowly missing Professor Billingham who had come to see Mr Wolverton. On his way to the library, he peered around the kitchen door.

"Morning," he said, sniffing the air. "That smells delicious."

Mrs Rose smiled as she looked up.

"Morning, Professor, and before you ask, yes that is fresh bread you can smell, would you like some with your morning tea?"

"Now, how could I ever turn that down, even though I am supposed to be trying to lose some weight? You wouldn't happen to have any of that wonderful jam?" chuckled the Professor as he brought his hands up and rubbed his big round potbelly.

Mrs Rose roared with laughter.

"Head down to the library. I will bring it down shortly; you're in luck as I have just made a new batch."

Inhaling the lovely smell once more, he turned and headed off to where Mr Wolverton was waiting impatiently for him.

In the garden, Sabella was busy preparing her kite. Running along carelessly, she gave the string a sharp tug as it soared into the air, rising high on the warm, early morning breeze. Now twelve years old, Sabella was tall, with long dark brown hair that always got tangled in the breeze and had piercing blue eyes that shone in the bright morning sunshine. She was beautiful and growing into her mother, Mrs Rose.

Ashlee, her sister, was slightly plump in her appearance with a head of thick red hair and dark hazel eyes that on occasions were almost black. They were different in so many ways and although Sabella loved her private schooling from Mr Wolverton, Ashlee always seemed incredibly keen to learn at every spare moment. She spent most nights reading marine biology books which were Mr Wolverton's favourite subject as he had a doctorate in the field. His father and grandfathers before him had always taught in the gatehouse.

Was this because Castle Cove sat miles away from the nearest town or school? Or maybe there was another reason? Whatever the reason, it was a magical place to be educated in and for Sabella to grow into herself.

As the sun climbed its way high into the vivid sky, the wind calmed down and Sabella's kite slowly made its way back down towards her. Walking to the end of the garden that had no fence or boundaries, she sat down on a rock gazing out to sea.

Old Mr Brooks' farm sat two miles away from anyone, he kept a very strange breed of cow in the surrounding fields that Sabella had never seen before and was always transfixed by. He was unkempt and scruffy with a large round friendly face and his big ears were emphasised by the fact that he was completely bald. Always wearing turned down wellies, faded jeans with braces and a scruffy check shirt. Once a week, he would trundle across the field in his vintage, John Deere tractor with milk and eggs for the Rose family.

"Girls, we are going soon, come in and get ready," called Mrs Rose, appearing at the back door.

Sabella got up from where she was sitting making daisy chains and ran towards the house which sat high up on a mound overlooking Castle Cove.

It was many hundreds of years old and reminded her of an old church with gargoyles above every window; some appeared as angels, whilst others emerged to her as a devil figure. The house was so old with the most amazing chimneys; they sat in the middle of the roof looking remarkably like fire-breathing dragons. The front entrance was grand, almost as though you were walking into a church, made of solid oak which curved up into a point at the very top. The surrounding stone was carved with strange unreadable words and symbols depicting sea creatures. There was a mermaid, a woman with a sword, a ghostly figure which was alongside an army of fish-like creatures. At the very top of the door, was a demon with arms outstretched. Evenly spaced around the doorframe, were five circles with writing underneath each one. They must have been of great importance to the person who built the house as they were carved into the staircase, the walls and even the stone floors. Mr Wolverton would always tell her that the first owner was an artist who was rather eccentric.

Walking through the front door, she bumped into Professor Billingham who was hastily making his way out, sweating heavily with his remaining wisps of hair stuck to his head.

"Morning, Professor," Sabella smiled.

Not speaking, he brushed past her and hurried off. Sabella carried on down the hallway where she met her teacher coming out of the library. He also looked hot and bothered and was wiping sweat from his brow. On seeing her approach, he quickly pulled the door shut.

"Morning, Mr Wolverton; is everything alright?" Sabella asked curiously.

"Everything is fine my dear; we have just had a tough morning with a new experiment and the Professor just needed some fresh air. Now you run along and get ready, you're not to worry," Mr Wolverton replied, patting her on the head before walking off calling Ashlee's name.

14

Not convinced by his answer, she watched him walk away before returning her gaze back to the library door. Why was she never allowed in there, yet Ashlee was? What was so important and secretive? Something was going on behind that door and it played on her mind as she walked upstairs to gather her things for the beach. On the way back down, she met her mother at the front door who was waiting for her.

"We are going to go on ahead. Mr Wolverton and Ashlee will follow after us," explained her mother adding to her suspicions that something was going on.

Walking down from the house towards Castle Cove, which was four hundred meters away, Sabella put the strange happenings of the morning behind her. She looked at the cove bathed in sunshine against the five pieces of remaining castle wall that were being gently lapped by the waves. Sabella thought to herself, once there had stood an amazing building overlooking the sea, sat in a horseshoe shaped bay.

Even these remaining pieces of wall were impressive, standing some twenty feet high and being at least fifteen feet thick. One part even had steps which she could still walk up. The strangest thing was that no one knew anything about the castle, when it was built or pulled down and no pictures or paintings had ever been found. All you could see of a once great castle were the five pieces of old stone wall that sat in the middle of the cove.

Climbing down a bank, Sabella and her mother laid a blanket out on a small patch of sand.

"I'm going down to the water, Mum."

"Okay, but remember to be careful; the tide is going out and the seaweed will still be wet and slippery," said Mrs Rose who was ever so slightly nervous about the simplest of things where her girls were concerned.

With the water receding, all the rock pools were now exposed and Sabella loved nothing more than searching for sea creatures. Grabbing her net, she moved from pool to pool finding small fish and crabs. She would never hurt any creature and once she had looked at them, she always returned them back to their pool or under a rock.

Looking up she saw that Ashlee and Mr Wolverton had arrived. Expecting her sister to join her exploring rock pools as she always did, she was mystified and puzzled to see her walking off to one of the largest pieces of castle wall which had worn out steps. She climbed all the way up before sitting down on the very top. Standing up from where she was, Sabella beckoned Ashlee to join her, but Ashlee's gaze remained intense looking out to sea. How curious it seemed to her, as any other day they would be racing each other to reach the sea first.

It was lunchtime so Mrs Rose called out, waving for her to come and have something to eat. Walking up the beach, she noticed that Ashlee was still sitting on the top step.

Sabella sat down on the tartan patterned blanket which had an open wicker basket in the middle filled with lovely, square cut sandwiches, egg and cress, cheese and tomato – which had gone a little soggy around the edges – and her favourite fish paste and cucumber. All washed down with a big glass of dandelion and burdock, and to finish off her mum's homemade cupcakes with extra icing. Looking at her mum who was staring at Ashlee and who looked like her thoughts were elsewhere, she tapped her on the arm.

"Mum, what's wrong with Ashlee? Has she done something she shouldn't have?" asked a concerned Sabella, trying to get her mother's attention.

But her mother just stared ahead.

"Mum," she called a little louder. This time she turned her head.

"Yes, dear? What's the matter?" Mrs Rose seemed anxious in her voice at trying to come up with a reason that Sabella would believe.

"Ashlee, what has she done wrong?"

Her mother stared at her for a few seconds and said, "Well, yes she's done something that she shouldn't have, and her punishment is to sit there all day and to not spend time with the family. But let's not talk about that now. Finish your cake, it's your favourite."

Mrs Rose turned her head and stared straight back at her sister.

Spending the afternoon swimming in the sea, Sabella couldn't think of anything her sister might have done to warrant this punishment. She kept swimming up and down the cove trying to attract Ashlee's attention but all she did was continue to stare straight out to sea.

As she went past one of the pieces of wall, she caught a glimpse of someone on the bank overlooking the cove. Not to make it obvious, she swam on until she was behind the next section of wall, holding onto it, she peered out to see if she could make out who this mysterious person was. To her surprise she saw it was the Professor and he too was now staring at her sister, along with her mother and even Mr Wolverton who was himself now taking a keen interest in her. What was going on? Not once did anyone look to see if she was safe, she could have been swept out to sea and nobody would have noticed. Something was going on, Ashlee was not in trouble, nor had she done something she shouldn't have and this was no punishment. Whatever it was, it was serious enough for her mother to be acting strange and most of all to be telling her lies.

From then on, she decided not to ask any more questions and to act like nothing out of the ordinary was going on. So when her mother called her in from the sea and they walked up together from the cove without her teacher and Ashlee, she didn't mention it.

Back at the house, Sabella went straight up to her room while her mother prepared dinner. Peering out of her bedroom window she could see the cove and its walls but it was hard to make out Mr Wolverton or her sister. Remembering her mother kept a pair of binoculars in the sideboard drawer at the end of the hallway, she went off and retrieved them. Back at her window, she lifted them up to her eyes and adjusted them into focus. Her teacher and sister were clear to be seen and they had now been joined by the Professor. The two men stood on the wall and Ashlee stood up on the top step. Strangely, they kept beckoning her forward onto the wall then pushing her back. This went on for at least an hour and her sister looked like she was getting upset as she was waving her arms around a lot and appeared to be shouting. Not long after, it appeared that whatever was going on had now finished as she watched the three of them start to walk back up from the beach towards the house.

Getting bored, Sabella scanned around with the binoculars, starting with the horizon she slowly moved down across the cove and its walls, then up through the fields towards the house. Suddenly, she dropped them to the floor and jumped back breathing heavily. She slowly crept forward and gently pulled back the corner of the curtain. Looking out onto the field she was convinced she had just seen the farmer Mr Brooks staring up at her, oddly there was no sign of him. Opening the window, she peered left and right, craning her neck but she couldn't see him anywhere. Feeling a little frightened, it was suddenly made worse by the loud knock on her door.

"Sabella, I have been calling you, your dinner is ready," said Mrs Rose sharply, which was unlike her she thought to herself.

"Okay, Mum, sorry I'm on my way," Sabella quickly jumped down the stairs.

Composing herself she walked along the hallway to the dining room. Sitting down at the table with her mum they were joined by Mr Wolverton, her sister and the Professor who had all finally, arrived back from the beach. They all sat down in silence and quickly ate their food before making their excuses of leaving the table to head down to the library together, locking the door behind them. Mrs Rose hardly touched her dinner and seemed very upset and preoccupied. Looking across the table she was half expecting to answer a barrage of questions from her daughter, but to her surprise there was silence.

"Is everything alright, dear?" her mother asked inquisitively.

"Everything is fine, Mum. Can we go back down to the cove again tomorrow?" Sabella tried to appear as though the day's events had not happened.

"Yes, of course we can," Mrs Rose replied slightly taken aback by her daughter's question.

"Also," said Sabella with haste.

"Yes," her mother replied ready to smooth over the strange happenings of the day.

"May I go to my room now and be excused? I'm in the middle of reading My Iron Island, and I'm also a little tired from swimming all day," Sabella looked out the window as she spoke to her mother.

Taking the opportunity to get her daughter out of the way she excused her from the table and started washing up.

Going down the hallway Sabella paused to look at the closed library door before continuing up the stairs. Pushing her door shut she laid on the bed and opened the book she was reading but it soon became obvious that other things were occupying her mind. What was going on? Why was everyone around her acting so strange? She had to think up a plan. Maybe she could sneak along to Ashlee's room and take a look around or maybe wait until everybody had gone to bed. With all these thoughts and ideas going around in her head, she slowly drifted off to sleep.

What she thought had been a restless night, Sabella sat bolt upright in bed, focusing her eyes on the clock she realised only an hour had passed but something had woken her. Looking towards the window she saw the sun had just set and there was a strange noise coming from the garden. Swinging her legs down she walked over to the window and much to her surprise farmer Brooks was in the garden. He looked straight at her and beckoned for her to go down. *Maybe he needed a hand with his cows?* Sabella thought.

Closing her bedroom door, she crossed the landing, passed Ashlee's room which was still empty and crept downstairs into the hallway. She could hear her mother in the lounge with the TV on and could see that the door to the library was still shut. By the time she had walked to the front door, Bosen had joined her. Turning the big key, she opened the door and stepped out into the cool evening air, shutting the door behind her. Turning around, she expected to see Mr Brooks but to her amazement there was no one there.

Walking alongside the house and past the window to the lounge where her mother sat, she looked out onto the field where the cows were happily laying down under the starlit sky. Could this day get any stranger? Sabella decided that she should go and get a good nights' sleep, and that she was still half-asleep. Hopefully, everything in the morning would be back to normal.

Heading back towards the front door she was suddenly stopped in her tracks by a very bright light beaming through a crack in the curtains from the library. This was going to be a good chance to take a peak as she tiptoed up to the window. Sabella peered in. Inside the room she could see her teacher, sister and the Professor all gathered around a chest with a very bright light coming from within it.

The two men were talking with raised voices like they were arguing, Ashlee looked upset and scared. Sabella could hear odd things being mentioned; a black cloud getting bigger, an orb and a doorway in the cove. The stairs on the wall were mentioned many times and that Ashlee should pass through before it was too late. Through fear of being seen and caught for eaves dropping, she hurried back around to the front door, sneaked in and headed up into her room, gently closing the door behind her. Lying on her bed, she thought about all the things she had just seen and heard before falling back into a restless nights' sleep of strange dreams.

The sun of a new day slowly crept its way over the horizon and bathed the house in an orange glow. Sabella found herself stood on the top step of the wall and looked at the long shadows they were casting along the beach. She had no idea how she had come there. She had been awake on and off all night trying to find answers to all the questions going around in her head. Was it all a dream or was there really a secret door hidden here?

Being an early riser, Mrs Rose walked across her room and pulled back the curtains to let the morning light in. Adjusting her eyes to the brightness, she could make out someone on the top step of the wall with long, flowing hair. "Sabella," Mrs Rose shouted.

"Please don't let it be, Sabella," running along the landing in a panic she threw open her daughter's bedroom door to find the bed empty.

"No!" She cried as she fled down the stairs and out of the front door. "Sabella no," Mrs Rose shouted at the top of her voice.

Sabella took one more step, and disappeared.

Chapter 3

Facing out to sea, Sabella felt the warm sun on her face. With her eyes tightly closed she thought to herself just how strange the last few days had been. It was impossible to ever think that there would be an invisible door leading to a strange, mysterious world.

Slowly, she opened her eyes and smiled for in front of her was a vast stretch of open sea. Looking down at her feet Sabella stood on the old stone castle wall but something was different; it was no longer in a state of ruin. Turning her head, she followed the stone wall to see that there were no longer five separate pieces, just one long stretch of wall sitting in the middle of the cove.

As Sabella spun around, she stumbled almost falling into the water. Right before her eyes stood the biggest surprise of all, a castle of grandeur towering above her, protecting itself with high stone walls and overpowering towers. Grass banks led up to the magnificent fortress that had appeared in Castle Cove. Sabella felt as though she was in a dream floating along in a surreal world waiting to wake up.

The gentle breeze swayed the brightly coloured flags flying high from each of the four turrets. Giant figures that looked like guards paced along the castle wall on lookout, clenching bows, arrows and swords, but what were they waiting for that needed such a presence to be felt? Sabella wondered.

The castle gave the impression as though it was almost touching the skyline, so powerful in its appearance. A drawbridge led from the outer wall down onto the beach, but how had it come to be here? Maybe there was a door after all that Sabella had stepped through. Stretching out her arms she stood on the top step to see if anything would happen by reaching out, trying to feel if there was a doorway in front of her. But there was nothing.

All of a sudden, the drawbridge slowly began to lower. Panicking, she quickly dived down onto her front as she had no idea of what was about to appear was friendly. The bridge hit the sand and Sabella slowly raised her head to get a better look. A strange looking horse and rider came charging out from under the archway which headed up the unmade road towards the gatehouse. Looking a little harder, she could clearly see that the gatehouse was the home she knew and loved which was identical in every way.

With the drawbridge going back up, Sabella decided to make a run for it, she knew her mother would have the answers to it all as she did to everything. Jumping to her feet and heart racing, she carefully made her way down onto the beach and ran across the sand with the walls of the castle towering over her. As she passed the front entrance, looking back she heard a voice.

"She's here; lower the drawbridge," shouted the gatekeeper who was peering out through the thick wrought iron gates.

With her heart pounding she took to her feet and ran for her life. Sabella heard a loud bang which told her the drawbridge was lowering once more. Fearing at the thought of looking back, she ran up the dirt track and burst through the front door of the house, she landed in a heap on the floor, where she was greeted by a bellowing laugh and booming overpowering voice.

"Well, hello there, young Sabella, I am very pleased to see you."

Who was this familiar voice to her? Looking up, Sabella was shocked to see Mr Brooks standing in front of her.

"Where's my mother? What are you doing here and why has a castle appeared in the cove out of nowhere?" said Sabella sharply, breathing rapidly as she fought through her words of confusion. "What's going on?"

"Be patient, so many questions young lady and so little time to explain everything," replied Mr Brooks as he turned and headed off into the kitchen. "Come on, we have lots to talk about, Sabella."

Picking herself up off the floor, Sabella looked out the door towards the castle where she could now see hundreds of people looking up towards the gatehouse. Hurrying into the kitchen and pointing out of the window she asked:

"What are those people doing out there? And why are they dressed in strange clothes?"

Turning around, Mr Brooks smiled saying, "They are waiting for you, Sabella."

"But why are they waiting for me? I don't know who they are," Sabella questioned, as she was feeling like she hadn't woken up from a dream.

"Because my dear you are their sorceress," said Mr Brooks.

"I'm their what?" Sabella burst into tears. "I don't understand any of what is happening, why is everything so different to me? I want it all to end."

"That I'm afraid is impossible. This is where you are meant to be. We have been waiting for you. They believe you are the protector of this kingdom, we need you Sabella and we are in great danger," replied Mr Brooks trying to be calm and as a matter of fact with Sabella, feeling upset and confused for her.

"But I still don't understand," cried Sabella.

"Sit down and I will tell you as much as I can," said Mr Brooks, confidently.

Sabella pulled out a chair, the very same one she used for breakfast every morning.

"Now firstly, you should know my name is Tobias, not Mr Brooks and I am your protector," he told her with a sense of haste in what he was saying.

"Yes but," said Sabella interrupting.

"Please wait I know it's all so hard to understand but I will answer all your questions in time. One more thing please stop your crying as you are burning holes in my table," said Tobias in a serious manner.

Shocked, she looked down and sure enough her tears had burnt clean through the wood. Looking back up she wiped a tear from her eye and held it up to the light, watching as it slowly dripped from her finger, landing on the end of a knife which lay on the table. It fizzed and bubbled before melting away.

"This is fantastic, it really is, please don't be upset," said Tobias.

"You seem just as powerful as your mother, which is a gift."

"My mother? What has she got to do with all this?" Sabella queried staring across at Tobias.

"Your mother was the head sorceress and she was born with the powers that will now pass to you, my dear," Tobias paused, "Your mother was head sorceress and ruler of Castle Cove. She was protector of all until your father was killed in the last great battle with evil. In her grief, she never wanted to be parted from you and your sister so she found a way all three of you could pass through the door into the other realm."

"What do you mean other realm?" Sabella asked.

"As you know the place you call home is a teaching school run by Mr Wolverton. All those who are destined to be a head sorceress are sent there through the door to learn about the planets, the orbs and creatures of the deep. Eventually, they are called back to take over as ruler and protector of this realm. But one thing does concern me deeply. It should be, your sister Ashlee sat here in front of me and not you as only the next protector have the power to walk through the door. Which means, I'm sorry to be the one to have to tell you this, but there is a strong possibility your sister may be dead. I think you are here to rule as head sorceress in her place. I have had my suspicions all along. I always felt uneasy with Ashlee, there was always something disturbing me about her," said Tobias sounding quite alarmed by what was happening.

With tears welling up once more in her eyes Sabella looked up at Tobias, "My sister can't be dead. I have just seen her, you must be wrong; she was fine."

Tobias leaned forward across the table towards her.

"As sure as this world has good and evil in it, then your sister may well be dead."

"No, that can't be right, I'm going to find Ashlee and my mother," Sabella cried angrily.

Tobias banged the table with his fist, his voice a little more forceful this time. "That person who claims to be your sister is an intruder and if they have made it to the other side it means they are learning everything from Mr Wolverton. That puts your mother in grave danger and if whoever it is manages to get back through the door with the orb and the knowledge, they will have the power to defeat us all, condemn our kingdom and everything we know to eternal darkness."

Sabella looked on with sadness in her heart whimpering. "I just can't believe my whole life has been a lie and that my sister isn't who I thought she was; how is any of this even possible, it's not real. Was this what you wanted to tell me when you looked up to my window and beckoned me down last night?"

"That was not me, Sabella. Maybe it was Ashlee or should I say the chameleon warrior. I presume it wanted you to see and hear the conversation. Maybe it needed you to know about the door as it could only ever get back to our realm with your help. Without you it will forever remain on the other side. On Earth. So I'm sad to say it seems your mother has a chameleon warrior with her," said Tobias.

"That sounds very bad to me? She needs our help we must go to her; how do we go back?" asked Sabella trying to make some sense out of it all and worried for her mother.

"It's bad enough but nothing compared to how much danger we are all in, if it manages to get back through here. We need to get to the castle and speak with Marmaduke. We also need you to begin to understand the behaviour of the creatures you will be dealing with. I am sorry to say Sabella, that will be sooner than any of us anticipated," answered Tobias knowing the path that lie ahead only too well.

"Me?" questioned Sabella, her heart beating so fast.

"Yes, Sabella, you. You're the only one who can save us now," said Tobias with complete faith in Sabella's powers.

"I still don't understand any of this," said Sabella. "But I will do all I can to help, whatever it takes."

"Thank you," replied Tobias rising from his chair. "I will always be here for you Sabella, through it all."

Walking down the hallway they stepped out of the door of the gatehouse. Looking down the hill, Sabella noticed a sea of people still standing outside the gate, waiting to catch a glimpse of her. They were cheering and holding petals from the land to lay down as a path in front of her.

"Mr Brooks, I mean Tobias are they good people?" Sabella asked.

"Good?" Tobias laughed. "These people are your people, you command them, they are loyal to you young Sabella."

As they slowly walked down the hill, seeing the arrival of their new sorceress made the crowd sweep inside the castle walls. Once reaching the entrance, Sabella stopped in amazement for there wasn't hundreds but thousands of people lining her path up to the steps, each one waving and cheering, throwing flowers towards her. She couldn't believe her eyes that they really were her people.

"Are you ready to greet your people?" asked Tobias as he held out a comforting hand.

Looking up Sabella smiled, took a deep breath and walked forward under the arch which overshadowed them. Turning, she caught a last glimpse of the old stone wall before the drawbridge slammed shut making her feel a little uneasy. Bending down Tobias whispered in her ear.

"Don't worry you are safe here, just smile and wave to your people they are so happy to see you."

Trusting his words, she did as he asked. It took them some time to reach the steps. Climbing to the top, she turned and gave a nervous wave.

"Now that wasn't too bad was it," said Tobias.

They both walked through the front entrance into the castle. The cheering and noise were now replaced with silence, all that could be heard was water as it ran down the walls underneath the walkway on which they were standing. Columns lined the passageway that opened up into a room at the end. Each column stretched from floor to ceiling, containing butterflies of such beauty that gave off a glow, fluttering their wings as she walked on by. Sabella was silenced by the bizarre sounds and dazzling colours she was seeing for the first time.

As they slowly approached what looked to be an important room, she looked up into the darkness, to a domed ceiling where thousands of lights shone back at her with every colour you could imagine. Standing in front of her, was a fountain with turquoise blue water that echoed around the room.

Two grand staircases swept around in an arch joining at the top forming a mezzanine walkway to the domed ceiling. The floor was laid out like a map of the oceans, showing the great seas of wonder and faraway islands. There was also something very familiar to Sabella, laid into the floor were round circles with strange writing inside them, like those at the gatehouse. Sabella counted four in total.

"Welcome, Sabella," a voice echoed around the room making her jump.

"Who was that?" Sabella asked looking around puzzled.

"Who was what?" said Tobias. "I didn't hear anything."

"Someone just called my name."

On looking up she noticed someone at the top of the stairs. "Look up there, Tobias," Sabella pointed.

"That's Marmaduke, he will be the one to teach you all you need to know from here," said Tobias with a half-grin, squinting his eyes.

"He looks very old, even older than you, Tobias," Sabella said as she watched the frail old man hobbling down the stairs on two sticks, his hair and beard almost touching the floor.

A voice then whispered in her ear.

"Never trust in anyone's appearance!" said Marmaduke.

Sabella leapt in the air as she let out a scream and saw that the old man was right behind her.

"How did you do that?" Sabella asked completely bewildered that he had moved so fast without her noticing.

"That Sabella, can be lesson one. Never and I mean, never trust in anyone's appearance, looks can be very deceiving and can hide something or someone very dangerous. Just look at the creature who you thought was your sister. It fooled everyone. You must be guarded at all times and expect the unexpected," explained Marmaduke needing Sabella to understand the most important and valuable lesson of all.

Staring at Marmaduke, Sabella noticed that his lips were not moving while he spoke to her.

"How are you doing that?" Sabella asked inquisitively with a half-smile that she was being fooled, or maybe this was another lesson.

The old man smiled, "Through telepathy, only you can hear me and what I have to say."

"That's amazing, so you mean Tobias can't hear us either?" asked Sabella in total disbelief of what she was seeing.

"Not a word, look I will show you. Tobias you are a fat overweight oaf. See nothing," Marmaduke replied chuckling to himself.

"Now Sabella, take his hand."

Reaching out she grabbed Tobias by the hand.

"Now this time it will be different. Tobias you are a fat, overweight oaf." Marmaduke was trying to remain serious in his delivery of an insult that was quite humorous to everyone except Tobias.

"Hey I heard that," grumbled Tobias as Marmaduke laughed.

"Wow that's fantastic, can I do that too?" Sabella asked.

"Of course you can my dear you are more powerful than you think and from tomorrow your training will begin but right now I sense you are both hungry and tired so it's time to rest," explained Marmaduke hastily, needing Sabella to rest and regain her strength for the days that lie ahead for them all. He knew she had to be strong.

"But I have so many questions and I'm not in need of rest, can't we start now?" questioned Sabella, as she could not shut off from what was happening around her.

"No," replied Marmaduke. "It is good that you are keen to learn but now you must rest."

Before Sabella could argue any more, he had gone. She spun around to look but he had vanished.

"How did he do that," Sabella asked Tobias who smiled and let out a loud laugh. "So many questions Sabella, you are the spitting image of your mother." She asked the very same things when she was standing where you are now. They will all get answered but not at this moment in time. "Come on let's go," said Tobias ushering Sabella to rest.

The pair made their way up the winding staircase to a large door at the top. Tobias pushed a blue button and the door slid back revealing a lift.

"This is where I leave you now Sabella, but if you need me at all, just call for me and I will come straightaway."

"This all seems…" Sabella was confused and lost for words.

Tobias butted in. "Strange, just a dream and you still don't understand all of it?"

"Yes," nodded Sabella.

"Don't worry it will become clearer day by day, but for now you are safe in your castle, so you must go and rest," said Tobias as he ushered her in the direction he needed her to go.

Tobias turned and walked down the stairs looking around, and when he got to the bottom, he gave Sabella a wave in the hope that she would feel she was not alone. Waving back, she watched him walk along the corridor until he was out of sight. Feeling nervous and a little scared she stepped into the lift and pushed a green button which made the door shut straightaway. There was a small jolt as the lift moved off. It was not like any lift Sabella had been in before, for it had the feeling of being in an enclosed cage, with a floor and a roof with open sides. So as it moved slowly up, she could see the walls brightly lit with thousands of gemstones lighting her journey. Up and up she went until there was another jolt, the lift stopped and the door slowly opened once more to let Sabella out. She gazed upon the room she entered into; it wasn't like anything she could have imagined. None of the walls were square; instead they gradually sloped up to the ceiling reminding Sabella of being inside a cave rather than a castle. She noticed there were also no doors, just an opening leading into the next room. Walking forward, she reached out touching the walls; they seemed to have strange patterns and textures carved into them which looked remarkably like the scales of a dragon or even a sea serpent. Also etched into them were more strange looking symbols that Sabella did not recognise. The next part of the room had the same curved walls but this time with windows on three sides to let in the light. There appeared to be a huge bed for her, it was covered with a patchwork blanket with even more strange looking symbols on it. Was it protection? What did all this mean? Sabella had so many questions. She walked over to it and tested its springs, yawning at the thought of climbing into it. Turning around, she looked at all the pictures on the walls of sea creatures from the ocean and faraway planets; some even showed the gatehouse, the cove and its wall.

Sabella gazed back towards the lift and saw a rickety staircase, she hadn't noticed it before. Walking over to it she peered up, it looked very dark up there. Sabella felt curious and brave enough to take a look. Slowly, she climbed the stairs creaking with every step she took, finding it very steep and narrow. Each step had a dip in the middle and she wondered who had previously walked this staircase, maybe even her mother. Nearing the top, a sapphire glow lit up the room like someone had just turned on a light. Sabella felt a presence and started to shudder.

"Hello, is anyone there?" Sabella called but no answer came back.

Carefully, she stepped into the room and she felt a sense of being in a cave once more but instead of one light in the centre of the room, it had hundreds of sparkling lights like a night sky. Edging closer for a better look, she realised they were not light bulbs but glow-worms. Each had its own little hole to live in, if they detected someone entering the room they would pop out and glow brightly.

As Sabella looked closer, she noticed so many books around the room, reminding her of the library she had done many hours upon hours of study in. Fish tanks full of unusual looking creatures, unlike any she had ever seen before, even in her books. What were these creatures Sabella asked herself?

The room had a desk at the far end which looked out of the window. Laid out were odd-looking charts and maps with the skull of a fish-like creature and a picture of a man. She picked the picture up and had a closer look, wondering if it was someone she would come to know, or could it be a friend of her mother's. Letting out a yawn, she put the picture back on the desk in the exact spot she found it.

Feeling tired and hunger taking over after the strangest day of her life she made her way back downstairs, watching the room resume to darkness as the glow worms returned into their holes. Once at the bottom of the stairs she looked around.

"That's odd," Sabella muttered. "There isn't a kitchen, how am I supposed to eat?"

She knew she hadn't missed anything, any rooms, stairs or hidden doorways. Thinking it was downstairs she headed back to the lift but on the way, Sabella suddenly noticed a long flexible tube coming from the wall. It had a funnel on the top with what looked like a giant cork stuck in the end. There was also a sign next to it which read, 'talk tube' and a list of names underneath. Reading down the list she noticed Tobias' name, so she grabbed hold of the tube and pulled it down to her mouth.

"Hello is anybody there? Can anyone hear me?"

Realising that the cork plug had to be pulled out, she gave it a sharp tug, and it popped out and fell down swinging back and forth on its chain from which it was attached. She then tried talking again.

"Hello," but still there was silence so she re-read the sign again, this time seeing that it said at the bottom to whistle down the tube the right amount of times in order to speak to the person you wished to speak to.

Looking along for Tobias' name, she noticed it said five whistles, so holding the tube close to her mouth once more, she did as it said. A voice came back at her this time.

"Hello, Sabella; it's Tobias. Is everything alright?"

"It's fine, thank you," she replied. "I'm just a little hungry and don't seem to have a kitchen in my quarters."

There was a laugh from the other end.

"Sorry Sabella, I was meant to tell you, all you need to do to get food is call Jester your servant," answered Tobias almost forgetting the smallest things he took for granted Sabella would not know.

"What? I have a servant too?" she gasped.

"Yes," Tobias laughed again. "I think he is number two on your list and will bring you all you need."

"Thank you," said Sabella.

Looking at the list, she saw that Jester was indeed number two so she whistled down the tube twice and jumped a little as she heard the lift start to move down. Pausing briefly for a moment before coming back up, she thought to herself she had never had a servant before. Now all of a sudden, she had a servant, a castle, and even a kingdom in just one day. The lift stopped and the door slid open, and instead of a tall man dressed in black holding a silver tray of food, like she was expecting, Sabella was looking down at a small robot, not standing more than four feet tall. He was made of brass and copper, held together with big screws which were all polished up to a high shine. It looked like an old diver's helmet with a porthole in the front which was his round eye. For his size, he had overly large hands and feet but Sabella couldn't help thinking how sweet he looked. Leaning forward, she held out her hand.

"Hello, Jester, my name's Sabella."

The little robot lifted his arm and shook her hand.

"Pleased to meet you, Miss Sabella," Jester replied in a very normal voice which came as a surprise to her. If her eyes had been shut, she would have been convinced he was human.

"Please just call me Sabella," she laughed.

The little robot looked back at her, his big eye blinking. Sabella had the strangest feeling, like she could tell exactly what the robot was thinking. He was smiling inside and she could feel it.

"Is there anything I can help you with?" Jester asked.

"Yes," Sabella answered. "How do I get some food please? I'm starving."

The little robot lifted his hand up to his chest, pushed a button and a flap dropped down.

"What would you like?" Jester asked, "Morning, lunchtime or evening meal?"

"Evening please," Sabella said holding her hand up to her mouth and giggling, hoping that Jester was about to go and come back a few minutes later with a lovely fresh hot meal. She hoped he didn't have one hidden inside his stomach. But if the last couple of days were anything to go by, she knew anything could happen and it did. She watched in amazement as a little yellow nugget rolled out onto the open flap. Jester picked it up and dropped it into Sabella's hand.

"Will that be all?" Jester queried.

"Well I was hoping for something a little bit more filling," Sabella said trying not to sound ungrateful.

"Is that not what you wanted?" Jester asked; his head dropping down in sadness at letting his mistress down on the first attempt.

Knowing she had upset him she placed a hand onto his shoulder. "No this will be fine," Sabella replied, lifting it up to her lips.

"Stop," said Jester. "You can't eat a golden nugget. First you must place it on a plate."

"Oh, sorry," Sabella said as she picked up a plate from beside her bed. "Now what?"

"Now hold the plate still, close your eyes and think of your most favourite food," said Jester.

Humouring the little robot, she did as he asked imagining a huge steaming plate of fish and chips. The plate in her hands felt a little heavier, so she quickly opened her eyes and there were the tastiest looking fish and chips she had ever seen.

"I'm not going to even ask how you did that, but it was amazing, who knew cooking could be so easy. I'm just going to enjoy every mouthful," Sabella said grinning.

"Will that be all? If so, I shall go now and return in the morning unless you need me before."

"Thank you, Jester," Sabella mumbled, her mouth full of food.

The little robot turned and walked off to the lift where he then disappeared. Sabella quickly finished eating feeling very full.

Stretching back onto the bed she pulled the cover around her and thought about home. No sooner had her head touched the pillow, she drifted off into a deep sleep.

Chapter 4

Falling to her knees, Mrs Rose stared at the steps. Tears were rolling down her face whilst questions filled her head. Crying Sabella's name, she sobbed in hope that her daughter would walk out from behind the wall, but she never appeared.

"Why?" Mrs Rose shouted banging her hands on the ground.

She slowly got to her feet and turned to look at the house before staring back at the wall. Walking towards it, she climbed down the bank, across the sand and up the steps, stopping as she reached the top. Turning to face out to sea, she extended her hand to try to open the door but nothing happened. The first question had been answered. She could no longer open the door which meant that she was no longer the head sorceress of Castle Cove. It also answered the second question which was: her lovely sweet daughter Sabella was her real successor and not Ashlee. The final one maybe hardest to take was Ashlee who was not her daughter after all but a chameleon warrior.

Mrs Rose looked towards the house and started to make her way back towards it, thinking to herself that Mr Wolverton would have all the answers. It had been such a special place to bring up her daughters, so peaceful and so safe. She had sacrificed so much to give them a different life, to escape the memories of losing their father during the last battle with one of Mortigan's evil armies.

Their father had given his life for them and secured the future of the kingdoms, knowing that Castle Cove was once again safe with Mortigan who was still banished to an icy tomb guarded by eternal sunshine. At least she felt safe in the knowledge that he could never escape and attack ever again, although the castle would always be under threat from his army. Lessons had been learnt and it was more than capable of coping with further attacks. So, when Mr Wolverton and Professor Billingham thought they saw darkness in the orb she never thought much of it, knowing it was impossible Mortigan could ever escape from where he was held captive.

So why was there a chameleon warrior here she thought turning her whole life upside down. It also meant somehow Ashlee must have been snatched in the last great battle and the chameleon warrior had taken her place. There was a very good chance that Ashlee would never be seen again, by now she was possibly even dead. Mrs Rose cried out, how could she not have known. For the first time in her life, she felt totally helpless having relinquished all her powers and magic the day she stepped through the door. To make matters worse, Sabella was now in a place she never knew existed and Ashlee who she loved had turned out to be a chameleon warrior and could well be the downfall to Castle Cove and all of its kingdoms.

Standing at the front door to the gatehouse she pushed it open and stepped in. Lost was the warm friendly atmosphere and sound of children, it was replaced by a cold lifeless feeling like the soul of the house had been taken away. Feeling alone and very scared for Sabella, she stood rooted to the spot listening to every slightest noise to indicate someone or something moving about. But all that could be heard was the tick-tock of the old grandfather clock which sat in the corner under the stairs. Reaching eight o'clock the chimes rang out around the house, sounding much louder than normal.

Looking first up the stairs, then down the hall to the library, Mrs Rose feared that the chameleon warrior might be in the house. She thought about going upstairs and tackling it alone as remembering her training as a sorceress, they were deadly assassins and capable of anything. As she crept down the hallway towards the library, each creak of the floor boards made her stop in her tracks for fear of alerting the warrior to her position. Reaching the library door, she gently tapped it, turned the knob and stepped inside. To her relief Mr Wolverton was sitting at his desk.

"Thank God you're here," she said quickly closing the door behind her and locking it.

"Whatever's the matter?" asked Mr Wolverton as he looked up. "Please come and sit down," he said gesturing to the chair opposite.

Walking over Mrs Rose slumped into it and put her head in her hands.

"Please tell me what has happened?" said Mr Wolverton leaning forward and resting his elbows on his desk.

Mrs Rose slowly lifted her head from her hands and looked at him "In all my years as head sorceress and all my training from you and your father counts for nothing."

"I don't understand," said the teacher looking slightly confused, "It's only the smallest of black clouds in the orb, I'm sure it's nothing. They haven't opened the door yet for Ashlee. So the Professor and I think it's happened before and is a false alarm so please don't concern yourself."

"Concern myself? It was me in my grief that I made the mistake of stepping through the door with my daughters putting Castle Cove in great danger. In my selfishness it was me and me alone who will bring the downfall of it all, and it will be forever in darkness. For when I stepped through the door, I brought with me not a daughter but a chameleon warrior," said Mrs Rose anxiously.

Rising from her chair she turned her back on Mr Wolverton and took a tissue from her pocket, wiping the tears that were now streaming down her face. Walking around the table the teacher put a comforting arm around Mrs Rose who turned to face him. He held the back of her neck in such a tight grip that it made her look up in pain, straight into the black lifeless eyes of a chameleon warrior. Before she had time to put up a fight, he plunged a knife into her stomach, pulling her close he whispered into her ear.

"Thank you, sorceress, for looking after me all these years but it is now time for me and the fire orb to return to Castle Cove, and for the dark ruler Mortigan to reign as king of all kingdoms and eventually all the universe. I have just one more job to do and that is to kill your daughter Sabella, then your family line is finished forever. I will then stand next to Mortigan in the destruction of everything and everyone. Darkness will rule; there is nothing you can do to stop it."

Releasing his grip from her, she fell to her knees and slumped on the floor. She watched as the warrior walked off to the corner of the room, where he picked up the box containing the orb of fire, before turning and walking back over to where she lay. Laughing, he then turned once more and left the library. With voices in the distance, the room was swirling around her and tears rolling down her face Mrs Rose closed her eyes and fell into darkness.

Chapter 5

Slowly opening her eyes, Sabella sat up. Staring at her over the end of her bed was one huge round eye.

"Good morning, Jester."

"Good morning, Sabella," replied the little shiny robot walking towards her with a tray in his hand.

"Is that breakfast for me?" she asked.

Jester nodded and placed the tray onto her lap lifting the lid.

"Oh, it's fish and chips again, and for breakfast, that's a little different," exclaimed Sabella.

"I thought you liked fish and chips. Can't you have them for breakfast?" asked Jester.

"Well you can, but it's not the normal thing you would eat at this time of day but it will do fine for now," Sabella said not wanting to upset the little robot. "But maybe we can try something a little different tomorrow if that's okay?"

Jester nodded in agreement. "I have run you a bath, put you out some fresh new clothes. Marmaduke has requested your presence in the main hall at nine o'clock. Please don't be late as he gets very angry."

"Thank you for all your help Jester, will you be coming back later?" Sabella asked.

"Yes, when you have finished your training, I will be back to serve you dinner." Jester replied.

"Okay, I will see you later then," Sabella smiled.

The little robot turned and walked to the lift, got in and disappeared.

Climbing out of bed, still dressed in her previous day's clothes, Sabella headed over to the window. It had been the strangest couple of days in her life but for some unexplained reason she felt very comfortable here, even to the point where she felt like she belonged. Looking out at the sun glistening off the wide expanse of sea she couldn't help but think of her mum, hoping that she was safe and wouldn't come to any harm from the chameleon warrior which was on the other side of the door. Even though she was in Castle Cove and so was her mother it felt like they were a million miles apart.

After freshening up in her amazing glow-worm lit bathroom, she tried to eat a little fish and chips which Jester had so kindly brought her for breakfast. Sabella prepared herself for her first day of training. She still had no idea who she really was, or why she was so important to Castle Cove, or even what she was being trained for but the next few days would hopefully give her all the answers.

Walking to the lift she felt nervous and even a little scared, pushing the button she opened the door and stepped in. With the door shut behind her she slowly descended until there was a slight bump and the lift stopped. Pushing the button once more she stepped out into the great hall. She looked around at this huge place with its star ceiling and map covered floor. Walking down the steps, she slowly made her way across the room studying the intricacy of the map with the islands, seas, ridges and trenches all clear to see. Right in the middle sat Castle Cove with a symbol of an orb on it, bending down she read the words, 'Fire Orb'. Sabella then had the strangest feeling that she was being watched but on standing and looking around she could see no one hearing only the running water. Putting her head down once more she continued to look at the map, following the path of a deep-sea ridge she came across another island called Brooknor. It also had a symbol of an orb. This one was called the 'Earth Orb'.

Hearing someone coming down the hallway, she stood up to see Tobias walking into view.

"Morning, Tobias," she said smiling as he made his way over and stood by her.

Just then something brushed past her making her spin around.

"Tobias, what was that? There is something in the room with us," said Sabella.

Before she got an answer, a shimmering figure started to appear, slowly at first but then as it became clearer it revealed a very long white beard and two sticks. Sabella let out a huge sigh of relief as Marmaduke appeared in front of her.

"I knew there was something in here with me," she said relieved.

"That's good, Sabella, you're sensing things already but it seems you have forgotten lesson number one. Do you remember what that is?" Marmaduke asked.

"Yes, I do remember you said to never trust anyone or anything," Sabella answered.

"Well done," said the old man. "But you have let your eyes deceive you and in turn you could have put your life in danger."

"How?" Sabella asked. "You are standing in front of me and Tobias is standing behind me so where is the danger?"

Marmaduke lifted one of his sticks and pointed behind her. Slowly turning around, she looked into the eyes of not Tobias but a chameleon warrior, who had transformed itself back from Tobias into its natural state.

Stumbling backwards she looked at the bulbous eyed creature with its rows of needle-sharp teeth. It was easily the ugliest thing she had ever seen, very tall like a skeleton. All covered in slimy translucent skin that you could almost see right the way through.

"What is that?" Sabella asked as she hid behind Marmaduke.

"There is no point hiding behind me Sabella for you will see many like these on your travels, you need to study them if you are going to survive the journey."

"Journey? What journey?" she asked.

"Never mind that now, we will come to that later on," Marmaduke replied. "He can't hurt you while you are here in the walls of the castle."

Sabella moved so she was facing the old man and could listen more intently.

"This creature is a chameleon warrior, the very same one your mother has with her on the other side of the door. I just hope that like her it also lost its powers when Mrs Rose took it through with her."

"What if not?" Sabella asked inquisitively.

"Well, let's not think about that now," Marmaduke replied avoiding telling her that her mother with no powers would be more than likely to have been assassinated.

"And what of Ashlee?" Sabella quizzed, "Tobias said she was dead."

"Tobias is right, I'm afraid Ashlee, the sister whom you came to love and played with all those years was the chameleon warrior. That's just how conniving and dangerous they are. Look I will show you," Marmaduke said turning around to face the warrior before commanding him to change, but the warrior just stood facing forward. Leaning a little closer he whispered.

"I will not ask you again warrior."

Again the creature remained motionless. Marmaduke jabbed one of his sticks into its leg. There was a bright blue flash and the warrior fell onto one knee. Marmaduke then jabbed the stick into its arm, the warrior cried out with pain.

"Stop, stop," shouted Sabella, "You're hurting him."

Turning, Marmaduke looked at her and in a calm voice explained:

"You have the potential to be a great sorceress, I sense you have amazing powers, but I am sad to say you have no concept of what you will be dealing with in order to save Castle Cove and all of its kingdoms. You will be battling against pure evil, the likes of which will test the skills and powers of any sorceress who has trained for many years. You have only a week to learn and understand the creatures. I will show you they all have but one aim and that is to kill you, everyone else and every living thing around us. It is a battle that has raged for thousands of years between good and evil, light and darkness and you Sabella are the key."

"Yes, but surely violence isn't the answer?" she asked.

Marmaduke paused for a while, dipping his head he let out a sigh. Looking back up at her he stared straight into her eyes. "You have a good heart, Sabella, for you are kind and you are good to others but this creature that is knelt before you is a killer. That's all, it is plain and simple, it has no heart or soul. It doesn't care about anyone or anything. When it looks at you all it has on its mind is to kill you."

Marmaduke walked away to the edge of the room and turned around.

"I can tell you are still not convinced. I wish I didn't have to do this but you need to understand."

Lifting one stick Marmaduke pointed it at the chameleon warrior a beam of light shot across the room hitting the creature. Immediately it stood up, turned its head and looked at Sabella who was quickly moving backwards across the room fearing something was about to happen. What happened next made her trip over herself, stumble and fall backwards onto the floor, for the warrior had changed from an ugly creature into her mum, then Tobias, and finally her sister Ashlee before reverting back to its ghastly self. Then in a blink of an eye it leapt through the air landing on top of her, pinning Sabella to the floor with one hand. Choking she looked up at the creature with its cold lifeless eyes, saliva dripping off its razor-sharp teeth and its deep growling of pleasure as it raised its hand up into the air to bring it down onto her. Closing her eyes, she prepared for the impact but it didn't come. The pressure had been released from her neck and the creature fell silent. Slowly she opened one eye, then the other and saw that the warrior was still poised to strike but that Marmaduke had replaced the spell upon it.

Coming into the great hall Tobias had just seen what had happened, running across the room he pushed the warrior over, picked Sabella up and looked across at Marmaduke with rage in his eyes.

"What are you trying to do?" Tobias shouted, "She has not been trained for this. She knows nothing of this place, its people or the magic so why are you subjecting her to such evil when she doesn't know how to deal with it."

Looking up at Tobias, Sabella gave him a reassuring smile. "I'm fine honestly Tobias, I needed to know." He looked back down at her. "It worries me for this is only the start. You have only met a chameleon warrior so far, there is a lot worse to come."

"Yes but at least I know now," Sabella said. Turning, she looked at Marmaduke. "Tell me all I need to know about the chameleon warrior and how I can destroy it."

Slowly, the old man made his way over to them, turned and looked at Tobias with the sternest of stares.

"You have never spoken to me like that before, your respect and tone of voice saddens me greatly. I have earned my place over many hundreds of years of teaching sorcery', you of all people should understand that. I would now like you to go; leave us in peace so we can continue training alone."

Dropping his head, Tobias knew he had done wrong. He turned and slowly walked down the corridor in disgrace.

"Please don't be too hard on him as he was only looking out for me," Sabella said.

"He cares for you greatly, Sabella, but he must not come in the way of your training. I am sure he will be fine. He just needs to go away and think about his actions for a while. I will speak to him later but meanwhile let's not waste any more time."

Turning around, he looked at the warrior who was still on the floor. Lifting one stick, he prodded it in the side, there was a flash of blue as he shouted at it to get up. Slowly, the creature got to its feet.

"Right, Sabella, as you know this is a chameleon warrior which is a creature that lives entirely on its own like a nomad. It travels around the vast oceans looking for work as an assassin; they are hired for their ability to be able to change into any form. To be a master of disguise, and of course, also to kill. Amazingly, they can also deal with sunlight which is something the other two creatures you will meet this week can't do which makes these even harder to detect. This one actually got within the castle walls and was sent to kill me but luckily I saw him before he managed to find me."

"I have a question," asked Sabella. "How can you tell who a warrior is?"

"That's a very good question, I was about to come to that myself. You have a gift just like me; you can tell if something has a soul or a heart. This creature standing before you has no such heart; it is a cold-blooded killer. Just feel its skin and you will see."

Sabella looked alarmingly at Marmaduke.

"Go on, it can't hurt you," he said.

Stepping forward she reached out and placed her hand on its arm. It was indeed slimy and ice cold but that wasn't all. Lots of evil images started to whirl around her head making her step back with tears welling up in her eyes at what she had just seen.

"Good, very good, you are opening up your mind and seeing these horrors that move around us. Now close your eyes, they will lie to you if you let them."

Sabella did as her teacher asked.

"Now in your mind's eye stare at the warrior. Focus all your energy on him and tell me what you see."

"Nothing," Sabella replied, "Just darkness."

"Look into the darkness for the warrior Sabella," Marmaduke asked.

"Wait I can see a shape, it's just an outline. But there is also something else there."

"What?" asked Marmaduke, "Tell me what you can see."

"There's another figure which is different, it's moving about."

"Follow it," he told her. "What does it look like?"

She carried on. "It has colour, an orange glow. I can also see a heart beating bright red."

"Now open your eyes, Sabella," Marmaduke told her excitedly.

Slowly, she opened them to find she had been staring straight at her teacher who had been moving around in front of her. He now had the biggest smile on his face.

"Your powers of detection are working fine and so soon in your training."

"Yes, but I feel so very tired now," Sabella replied.

"Practice, practice, practice, it all comes with practice," Marmaduke said, hobbling over towards her.

"The main thing is they are working and you can now distinguish between life and death, good and evil. You have done very well today, for the rest of it I would like you to study the maps of not only the oceans but also the stars as well. They are both very important to you, do not forget the books in your quarters. They will help you answer any questions that you may have on the chameleon warrior. They have been put together over many hundreds of years and hold a wealth of knowledge in them. Remember Sabella, what they are, also just what they are capable of."

Turning, Marmaduke prodded the warrior in the back and they went walking off down the corridor out of sight.

The hours rolled past, day turned into night, not that Sabella noticed as there were no windows in the great hall. She had covered most of the nautical map of the oceans remembering islands, seas, deep ridges and routes of passage until her eyes felt so tired and heavy that she could no longer focus on them. *Maybe, a change is better than a break,* she thought, so lying on her back she looked up at the stars shining back at her from the domed ceiling above. Sabella already had a good knowledge of the night sky having spent many an evening in the garden of the gatehouse with her mother, finding and naming the constellations. But she would be doing none of that tonight for within a minute of her lying down she was fast asleep.

With all the cleaning and tidying done, Jester was getting a little worried about Sabella as it was getting very late and there was no sign of her. Deciding he had better go check on her, he got into the lift and went down. Getting out at the bottom, he peered first left then right, but it wasn't until he peered over the edge of the stairway that he saw her flat out on the floor. Knowing no harm could come to her while she was in the castle, he guessed she must have fallen asleep. Walking over to her he placed a hand on her shoulder and gave her a gentle shake, but Sabella was in a very deep sleep and wasn't about to wake anytime soon. Not wanting to leave her there on the cold stone floor he carefully picked her up and slowly walked back up to the lift. Once in her quarters he placed her down on her bed and pulled her blanket over her. Being careful not to make a sound, he turned out the lights leaving her to rest.

Chapter 6

Morning broke, as Jester opened the blinds the sunlight came flooding into the room. Turning, he walked over to Sabella's bed to wake her but he found it empty and already made. Confused, the little robot looked around and noticed a faint glow of light coming from upstairs. Walking over he started climbing the stone steps. As he neared the top he could see Sabella sat at her desk.

"Morning, my little friend," Sabella said as her head popped up from behind a giant book.

"Good morning, Sabella," replied Jester walking over to the desk, having great difficulty seeing over the top of it.

"Thank you for putting me to bed last night, I woke up early so I thought I would do some reading on all the things I need to learn."

"Would you like some food now?" Jester asked.

"I thought you would never ask, I'm starving," Sabella laughed.

The little robot pressed the button on his chest and the flap dropped down, within a few seconds a little round nugget rolled out. Picking it up, he handed it to her.

"Do I need to do the same thing as before? Close my eyes and think of something that I like?" Sabella questioned.

The little robot nodded so Sabella closed her eyes and thought of the biggest bacon sandwich with lettuce and tomato just like her mother made, there it appeared in her hands. Tucking in straightaway, she finished the last mouthful whilst walking down towards the lift as she didn't want to be late meeting Marmaduke.

"See you later, Jester," she called out as the lift door shut, heading down.

Tobias was already there waiting when Sabella stepped out at the bottom, she was just about to call his name as he was facing away from her but she stopped herself. Maybe it was another trick that her teacher had set up she thought to herself, to try to test her. Gently stepping back, she closed her eyes, concentrating for a second or two. First there was just darkness but then gradually things started to happen. Objects started to appear in front of her starting with the stairs and walls, a few seconds later the rest of the room started to take shape. It was almost as if she were looking through night vision which could pick up on heat and movement. Slowly, she scanned around the room, what she first had thought was Tobias, when she stepped out of the lift it was clearly not. This person had no body heat, appearing just a black lifeless figure which could only mean one thing, it was a chameleon warrior disguised as Tobias.

Carefully making her way down the stairs with her eyes shut alongside her heart racing, she noticed two other figures with her in the room. Stopping she opened her eyes and adjusted them to the light but the figures disappeared.

Her teacher and Tobias had to have been the people in the room with her but under some sort of spell making them invisible to the naked eye. Sabella closed hers once more. She instantly picked them up hiding in the corner behind a pillar. Not wanting to give the game up too quickly she strolled around the room pretending to look around until she was standing right behind them. But still they didn't move.

"I can see you two you know," Sabella said.

"I told you she would be able to see us," laughed Tobias.

"I see you two are causing mischief," Sabella remarked as she opened her eyes to see both of them visible once more. "Wasn't I supposed to find you then?"

"To learn the skills of how to determine the difference between living and the dead usually takes years of practice, but for you to have seen us under an invisible spell shows that you have a lot of your mother's gifts," explained Marmaduke.

Turning, he hobbled over to the centre of the room and stood in the middle of the map.

"So Sabella tell me firstly, what it is you know about the orbs?"

"Well, I know there are four of them, each one is filled with an element essential to life, they have been placed on different islands. I also know that they are very safely hidden so it sounds almost impossible to find them, but I still don't know from what or whom they are being protected," Sabella replied.

"We will come to whom in a moment," replied Marmaduke, "First let me tell you about the orbs. There are in fact five orbs but many books only ever recognise the four that you have just mentioned, these being earth, wind, fire and water. These four make up everything that you can see around you, the air you breathe, the sun that warms your skin, the water you drink and even the ground that you walk on. The fifth one is called the dead of night, just like we need the four element orbs we also need a balance between good and evil, hence that is why we need the fifth orb. We are happy to live alongside evil but the keeper of that orb is not happy to live alongside us or anything for that matter.

His name is Mortigan, Sabella, he is evil in its purest form you must understand that. He never rests until this kingdom and every living thing on every planet that lights up the night sky in every galaxy and universe is bathed in darkness and death. The orbs themselves have amazing powers but only someone with a pure heart can control them. A heart of pure love or pure evil and only a person with one of those can summon the armies of the orbs. You, Sabella, have the orb of fire, but unfortunately it is on the other side with your mother as a signal for the current sorceress to return if there is danger, but also for safekeeping. As I said Mortigan himself has the dead of night orb but he has limited use of it at this time."

"What do you mean at this time?" Sabella questioned.

Marmaduke walked over to the very top of the map and beckoned for her to join him. Using his stick, he pointed to a big round island of ice.

"This place is called Stenbury, it is always bathed in sunlight all year 'round due to its location thus, stopping anyone or anything dead getting in or out. It is cold, barren and inhospitable and has become the prison of Mortigan held two miles under the ice in a ring of sunlight where he can never escape. Obviously, there is the exception of the chameleon warrior who can still move in the sunlight."

"So why is Mortigan a danger now to us all?" Sabella asked.

"Well normally the fire orb or any orb would tell us by showing a black cloud in its heart," said Marmaduke.

"I remember something I overheard one night about a small cloud in an orb. How did you find out?" Sabella quizzed wanting to know.

Marmaduke pointed at the chameleon warrior stood in the middle of the room

"He was sent to kill me, but once caught I could read his mind and I found out that Mortigan was planning his escape and further attacks on the kingdoms. We don't know how or when but we, or rather you cannot let it happen, he must be stopped. He must have found some way to stay in darkness, for the moment Mortigan steps out into the sun he will be immobile. That's why you Sabella must travel to Stenbury and make sure that he is kept in his prison forever."

"Yes, but I really don't think I'm trained to deal with all this Marmaduke," said Sabella with a frightened tone to her voice.

"None of us are but you are not alone. You will have the best people with you including Tobias," Marmaduke answered trying to encourage her.

Turning to Tobias, Sabella looked up at him and he gave her a big reassuring smile.

"Okay then, what now?" Sabella asked turning back to her teacher.

"Now, Sabella, you are ready to meet the viper warrior and the bearded dragon warrior. Please follow me," said Marmaduke.

The three of them made their way over to the corner of the room where Marmaduke lifted his stick, he proceeded to push four squares on the wall in a certain order, making a section of wall slide back revealing a lift, similar to the one she used in her quarters. Stepping into it, the wall slid back into place and they started to descend. The walls of the shaft started off the same as her bathroom, brightly lit with hundreds of glow-worms lighting their way but all of a sudden they turned to walls covered in wet moss, then to wet slime before finally ending up just thick black mould and fungus dripping with something that looked like snot. The light from the glow-worms had long since gone and was now replaced with candles that flickered in the foul smelling, musty air. The lift then stopped but not with the usual bump, more of a squelch as it came to rest at the end of a very long passageway.

Stepping out, Sabella looked around and listened to the sound of water dripping off the black mouldy walls. They couldn't go anywhere for in front of them was a large iron gate blocking their way down the passage. In the distance she could hear the faint noise of footsteps approaching, then out of the darkness appeared a figure walking towards them standing some three meters tall and nearly as wide. This person could barely fit down between the walls and had to walk with a stoop. Coming up to the gate she could see that he was not exactly what you would call human, only half, the other half was a robot. Even his face was split in two, showing he had half robot and half-human features. Putting a big key in the lock he turned it, opening the gate.

"Morning, sir, how are you today?" the giant asked.

"Very well thank you," replied Marmaduke, "Sabella, this is Keltal one of the dooadite twins, you will meet Kaylum in a moment. As you can see being so big only one of them can fit down the passageway at a time."

Stepping forward Sabella held out her hand to the giant who looked shocked at this gesture and turned to Marmaduke for guidance.

"Go on," Marmaduke nodded reassuring Keltal it was alright to shake Sabella's hand.

Holding out his hand which was easily as large as a shovel he bowed his head, "It is an honour to meet you sorceress and I look forward to serving and protecting you in the future," said Keltal feeling very privileged to be by Sabella's side.

"Well thank you, I feel a lot safer knowing I have you and your brother to protect me," said Sabella. "But please from now on only call me Sabella and no longer sorceress."

Looking up at the big giant she gave a smile and stepped aside. "After you please, Sabella," Keltal said in his booming deep voice.

Walking down the passageway the air became more and more stagnant and got harder to breathe. Reaching the end, she was confronted with another iron gate which this time was unlocked by Kaylum, the second giant twin. Sabella introduced herself to him noticing he was identical to his brother, apart from his left side being a robot, whereas Keltal's robot body was the opposite side.

Marmaduke turned to Sabella, "You know I said to you that every orb has an army?"

"Yes," Sabella replied.

"Well down here is where we keep two members of the dead of night army."

With Kaylum and Keltal on either side guarding Sabella, they walked over to where Marmaduke stopped in front of a piece of glass which stretched from floor to ceiling.

"In this tank Sabella we keep the viper warrior," Marmaduke said nodding to Tobias, who then flicked a switch, so that a special light came on that wouldn't affect the creature.

Expecting to see a big ugly vicious killing machine, she was very surprised to see a fish swimming around in the tank. Admittedly it was hideous, with a round face, slitting jet black eyes and a gigantic mouth-containing row after row of razor-sharp teeth.

"This Sabella is the viper warrior," Marmaduke explained. "They are supreme fighters, attack in armies of thousands, very loyal and will die for their master. They are fast, agile and highly trained in all forms of combat. They may only stand at a metre tall but don't ever under estimate these creatures; you will be seeing many of these on your travels."

Taking a step forward Sabella took a closer look at the fish swimming around the tank, "I must say it doesn't look as bad or as dangerous as the chameleon warrior."

"As I have said to you many times before looks can be very deceiving," replied Marmaduke as he nodded once more at Tobias who flicked another switch and the tank started to drain of water.

As the water reached the bottom of the tank the warrior transformed itself from a swimming fish with fins and gills, to a creature with arms and legs. Slowly, it stood upright and lifted its head so it was staring right at her. Stepping up to the glass it didn't take its eyes off of her once. It lifted its arms up and brought them banging down on the glass, the sound echoing around the room and off down the passageway. Then there was the most ear-piercing screech as it ran its long razor-sharp claws down the glass, cutting into it leaving markings.

"That's enough," said Marmaduke as Tobias flicked the switches back and the tank was once more pumped full of water returning the creature back to a grotesque fish swimming once again.

Sabella turned to her teacher. "Just when you think you can't encounter anything eviller, I can say that I saw the hatred in its eyes, it wanted to kill me of that I have no doubt."

"It would have killed us all given the chance," Marmaduke replied as they walked over to a second window of glass.

"So, this must be the bearded dragon warrior?" Sabella pointed out. "As you have left it to last, I'm guessing this is the worst one. I can't see how it could be though as it's hard to believe anything could be more evil in its manner than the two I have already seen."

Tobias looked over at Marmaduke who gave him the signal to switch the light on. Putting her hand up to her mouth, Sabella stifled a scream for this creature was huge, almost as big as the twins. It was a mass of rippling muscle so big that its skin jet-black in colour was pulled tight showing all of its veins. The warrior had a big round head that tapered down to a point at its chin, which in turn had long pure white whiskers hanging from it. Its eyes which were also pure white shone out against the blackness of its skin.

"Do not worry, Sabella," said Marmaduke stepping up beside her, "It cannot harm you for it is very much dead and is held in this tank of special fluid so we may study and learn from it."

"So what have you learnt so far?" Sabella asked.

"Well what we do know is that they are the personal bodyguards of Mortigan. We don't know where they come from or how many of them there are. You must understand that there are parts of the deep ocean that no one has ever been, places so dark Sabella and so dangerous that nobody would ever survive. Mortigan may have found them in a deep canyon which is in a remote part of a faraway ocean. That is something we may never know but the bearded dragon warrior is far too dangerous to keep alive, as they have the strength of fifty men, they move with amazing speed."

"So how do we kill them?" Sabella asked.

"The only known way is by sunlight for that is their only weakness we have found," replied Marmaduke.

"There is something I don't understand though," questioned Sabella.

"What is that?" asked her teacher.

"If sunlight is the only way to kill them then how did this one die? Surely being exposed to the sun would have turned it to a pile of ash?" Sabella questioned.

"She is right master," said Tobias, "There must be another way."

"Unfortunately, we may never know how this one died for the only person to witness its death died with it, which was your father," Marmaduke answered.

Sabella looked at Marmaduke and then back at the bearded dragon warrior. Walking up to the glass she stared at the creature before her. "My father must have been an amazing man, a true warrior. If he found a way to kill them then so must I."

Walking over to her, Tobias put his hand on her shoulder. "I think it's time we left here for now, don't you?"

Nodding in agreement the three of them turned and walked back up the passageway leaving the twins to lock the gates behind them. As the lift went up into the fresh air Sabella turned and looked at her teacher. "How did the twins come to be half robot?" she asked.

"They were born Siamese twins. They would have died if it wasn't for Professor Brumbles whom might I add will be on the ship with you on your travels. He is a great scientist and inventor of all that is mechanical or robotic in Castle Cove. He separated them at birth giving them a robotic side to replace the half they were missing. It took a great deal of time followed by extraordinary magic, but now they are fine men and great fighters themselves."

"Yes," replied Sabella, "I am glad that they will be accompanying me on my journey."

The lift stopped, the wall slid back and the three of them stepped out. Free from the foul-smelling pit below, they all gulped big mouthfuls of fresh air.

"You have seen all the creatures from the dead of night orb now Sabella, I know it's been a strange and bewildering few days for you but I am extremely proud of you. Your powers as a sorceress have amazed me. You might not know it yourself yet but you have a warrior's heart. Now, I will leave you to study as you don't have much time before you sail. Remember that I and Tobias are always here to answer any questions that you may have," said Marmaduke.

"I do have one question before you go," Sabella said. "How can you be so certain I have a pure heart?"

"All children born to a sorceress have the mark of the gods on the back of their necks and were born in the cave of the gods. These two things ensure your heart is pure and that you are gifted with the powers to protect us, the kingdom and the orbs from eternal evil," answered Marmaduke.

"I do have a birthmark on my neck, so did my mother and come to think of it, Ashlee had one too," Sabella questioned.

"You see," said her teacher. "Apart from Ashlee who we now know is a chameleon warrior, both you, your mother and all sorceress before are all born with the mark of the gods."

"If all this is true then where is the cave of the gods? Shouldn't I go there?" asked Sabella.

"Of course you can. In fact I was going to suggest you visited it before you set off on your voyage. Tobias will take you there tomorrow, it's not far away. But please until then you must study and I will see you tomorrow," said Marmaduke.

Marmaduke and Tobias walked off down the corridor leaving her once again to study the maps of the oceans and skies. Sabella was very excited about leaving the castle if only for a day, after being kept inside. It was an adventure to be had in her mind and hoped she would learn something that would later be of great use to her.

Chapter 7

Sitting bolt upright in her chair, Sabella rubbed her tired eyes. Putting her arms back on the desk where she had been sleeping all night, she lay her head back down on them and let out a groan at the thought of having to wake up. In front of her she could hear the familiar sound of Jester moving about. Peering over the top of her arms a big round eye looked back at her.

"Morning, Jester," Sabella grumbled.

"Morning, Sabella, are you alright this morning?" Jester asked.

"I'm just very tired, it's been a long night. I didn't get much sleep," Sabella replied.

"I think you had a nightmare for you were shouting in your sleep," Jester said.

"Was I? What was I shouting about?" Sabella sounding surprised when she asked.

"It was something about a big black wave and that danger was coming," replied the little robot.

"Oh I see, I can't remember anything about that maybe it will come back to me. What's the time by the way?" asked Sabella.

"Nearly nine," Jester replied.

"Oh no I'm going to be late," Sabella gasped as she rose from her chair, wobbling as she gave out a giant yawn on her way down to the lift. Sabella got in and continued down to where Tobias was waiting for her.

"Morning, Tobias," she said letting out a big yawn.

"I sense that someone's still a little sleepy," Tobias asked smiling to himself.

"Just a little I stayed up late last night studying. Where's Marmaduke?" Sabella asked.

"He will see you later when you return. He prefers to stay in the castle as he isn't really one for socialising with people or crowds. Now are you ready to go?" Tobias asked.

"Yes, I can't wait to go outside," Sabella replied.

Walking down the beautiful corridor towards the door at the end it felt like she had been in the castle for weeks even though it had only been a matter of days. As the door closed behind them Sabella looked out from the castle steps, she could see people going about their everyday life, a bustling market was setting up in the castle grounds with stalls trading their wares.

"These people have no idea the danger they could be in, do they?" Sabella asked.

"That's the way we like to keep it, these are normal everyday people who are kind and getting on with their lives. They entrust to us their protection and that of their kingdom," replied Tobias.

Walking down the steps they walked through the market as people stopped to stare at the stranger amongst them. Some were brave enough to speak to their new head sorceress. A couple of stallholders even gave gifts of jewellery, embarrassingly she accepted. Eventually they reached the main gate. There was a familiar noise as the gate opened up. Stepping out onto the beach she bent down and scooped up a big handful of sand, letting the grains run through her fingers she was standing on the very same stretch of beach that she played on through the summer walking her dog Bosen.

In front of her stood the first defence; the stone wall stretched the whole length of the cove. Sabella could see many men stood on top of it working amongst stacks of crates and barrels. Three masts towered over the wall stretching high into the air casting long shadows in the morning sun. Walking across the sand they climbed the stone steps up to the very top. Expecting to see or feel the magic doorway there was nothing, just the view of the sea. *It must be here somewhere*, she thought, holding her arm out and turning around.

"Come on, Sabella," Tobias called as he walked off without her.

Checking for a door one last time she started to walk towards him. It was a hive of activity with all sorts of items being loaded onto a huge ship called the Compton which sat moored up against the wall, and what an amazing vessel it was. The hull was jet-black made from what looked like steel plates, all held together with big rivets. The decks and tall masts were also black with one enormous red funnel which rose from the middle of the ship. It was powered by the wind and also had two big circular paddles, one on either side which meant it was powered by some other means as well. The wheelhouse, air ducts, railings and winches were all highly polished brass and copper that stood out from the shiny black hull.

Sabella stood and watched as hundreds of crates, barrels, food and equipment were loaded aboard. Most of the heavy lifting being done by the dooadite twins, who could easily carry a barrel under each arm or a crate above their heads. Turning to Tobias who was giving orders on how he thought things should be done, she asked. "Are we going to need all these supplies?"

"This is only half of it," Tobias chuckled. "We will be travelling to a very dangerous and inhospitable place. We don't know how long we will be gone for or what we will find when we get there. Though, in my experience you can never have enough equipment or supplies. Come on, let's go and leave them to it," Tobias said shouting a few last orders before turning and walking off along the wall.

Climbing down onto the beach which stretched off along the headland they started walking, the castle slowly disappearing behind them. Continuing on for half a mile more with the sun on their faces, the water gently lapping the shoreline, not having the pressure of studying, the castle, or Marmaduke they could relax. They talked about a whole range of things such as life back through the door, cows, the gatehouse, her mother and even fish paste sandwiches which made them both laugh out loud.

Eventually, they rounded the point, in front of them lay Rocken End, a small sandy cove ringed with low cliffs, in the middle sat a very large cave. That's when it finally sunk in and she realised that this was nothing like home. It was a different place altogether. Although the castle, house and bay looked the same everything else was totally different. The new world she had stepped into was a world away from the Castle Cove she had grown up in. As they walked a little closer, she could see torches on the walls, the flames flickering in the breeze causing haunting shadows to move across the walls and ceiling. Standing at the entrance to the cave, she noticed the torches stretched back as far as she could see. On the floor next to the cave's entrance a pile of new torches lay neatly stacked.

Tobias bent down and picked two up and lit them both, handing one to Sabella. "Ready?" he asked.

"Ready," Sabella replied.

The first thing she noticed as they stepped into the shadow of the cave was the temperature drop. It was so cold that the hair on her arms stood on end and sent a shiver down her spine. Gradually, as the natural light faded leaving them with only the light from their torches, so did the noise of the outside world. Slowly, it was being replaced with different sounds, of water dripping off the ceiling into pools causing echoes to bounce off the walls. Lizards and other creatures scurried away from their approaching torches and the sound of their footsteps as they walked towards the back of the cave. Steadily, the walls closed in on them until they were now standing in a small tunnel where there was no natural light. Without their torches they would have been standing in the pitch black.

Without really knowing why Sabella closed her eyes and focused on Tobias, using her new skill of checking if something is good or evil by its heart. She was relieved to see that Tobias had a very healthy glowing heart but that wasn't all. Her powers were becoming stronger by the day and now she could see other hearts also of the creatures that lived in the cave. Walking through a doorway at the end of the tunnel Tobias lit six torches which hung around the room they had just stepped into.

With her eyes open once more she looked at what lay before her. The room looked very familiar. Pillars of precious stones, sixteen in total, held up the ceiling. There were also the strange looking symbols on the walls mirroring what she had seen in the castle. Towards the back of the room she could see a big block of stone, approaching it, she noticed that the middle had been carved out.

"Tobias what is this used for?" Sabella asked.

"That is where the new born babies to the sorceress are laid when they are born," Tobias answered.

"So was I placed in there when I was born?"

"You were indeed and so was your mother and her mother before that," Tobias replied.

"So what do all the paintings and symbols mean on the walls? I have seen the same ones in the castle," Sabella questioned.

"No one really knows. They are very old and definitely part of your past, Sabella, and not the people who live here," Tobias answered.

"Why do you say that?" Sabella asked.

"Simply because these people don't possess the materials or the technology to create things such as these pillars, there is nothing in Castle Cove to explain the symbols. Someone must have written them on the walls. Maybe, it was one of your ancestors when they first came to Knighton," said Tobias.

"It's all very interesting, I would love to know what it all means," she asked.

"Maybe you should ask Marmaduke; he might be able to tell you some more," suggested Tobias.

"What about your past, Tobias?" Sabella asked.

"Like Mr Wolverton and the Professor, my ancestors and I were recruited for our skills as adventurers, explorers and also close guardians of the sorceress, who was your mother at the time."

"So do a lot of people on Earth know about my race and the door to Knighton?"

"No only a select few are chosen to assist you in the protection of the orbs. Anyway, people on Earth don't believe in another world and even if I did speak of all I know, which I never would, they would call me mad and say that Earth was the only planet with life on it. I think we should be going now," Tobias insisted.

Sabella nodded in agreement and followed as he led the way out of the room and back down the tunnel. Back at the entrance, they placed their torches up against the cave wall, blinking as they stepped out into the warm sunshine. They took a minute to let their eyes adjust before setting off along the beach back towards the castle and the wall which was still a hive of activity.

"How long are we going to be away for Tobias?" Sabella asked, worryingly.

"That I don't know for not many people venture that far north. It really all depends on the weather, if we get attacked on the way, and how bad the ice is when we get there."

"Hang on, you just said attacked?" Sabella queried, "What do you mean, Tobias?"

"Well as you know the dead of night is the minute either side of midnight which is the only time the dark army can attack us, but don't worry though that will only happen if we pass over a deep sea ridge for that's the only time it's dark enough for them to reach the surface. If all goes to plan, hopefully we will cross them during daylight hours. The Compton has been built to withstand any attack. She is the best ship Professor Brumbles has ever built; in fact she is so good it's the only one."

Reaching the wall, they climbed up the rocks and walked along to where the steps led down the other side. Stopping, Sabella stood at the spot where she had passed through the door. If only she could open it and step through to help her mother. Her eyes filled with tears thinking of her.

Turning, Tobias looked at her. "Are you alright, Sabella?"

"I'm worried about my mum for if she has lost her powers then she is at the mercy of the chameleon warrior and knowing the danger she must be in I fear the worst. I just wish I could step back through and help her."

"I'm sure she is fine, you have to concentrate on your kingdoms and the orbs now. Once all is safe here then you can step back through," Tobias said trying to reassure her in some way.

"Yes, but we don't know when that is going to be; and by then it could be too late."

"I know your mother, I know she would always want you to do what's right also put your kingdoms and your people first, wouldn't she?"

"Maybe you're right. I should do as she would if she were here, and I think she would want me to make sure all is safe first and fulfil my role as head sorceress."

"Exactly, now come on, Sabella, we better go you know how grumpy Marmaduke can get," Tobias said grinning broadly.

Stepping off the wall onto the top step, Sabella turned and whispered, "Hang on, Mum, I will come back for you I promise."

Chapter 8

Looking out from her bedroom window, Sabella stretched, aching from the previous day and night of hard training with Marmaduke; he had pushed her very hard as time was very limited. Watching her people, she thought how thousands of them were entrusting their survival in her as they had done with her mother and grandmother before. It had been a restless night as many thoughts of the unknown whirled around her head. Twice she had got up to talk to Tobias on the talk tube to clarify some things she couldn't understand.

As the sun slowly rose up over the horizon, she watched the ship being loaded with the last of the supplies. It was all slowly coming to life and lights could be seen in the wheelhouse.

Popping the last piece of toast dripping with melted butter into her mouth, that Jester had so kindly conjured up for her, she walked over to the lift stepping inside. Sabella looked around her apartment for hopefully not the last time taking a deep breath, the next part of her adventure was about to begin. Pushing a button, the door slid shut and she slowly descended.

Stepping out at the bottom, she found Marmaduke was already waiting for her. Standing at the top of the stairs, he was looking down at the map which was laid out before him.

"Sorry was I supposed to meet you this morning?" Sabella asked breaking his train of thought.

"No," he mumbled turning to face her, "I just needed to see you before you set sail."

"Was it something important?" Sabella queried.

"On the contrary, I just wanted to say how well you have done and how impressed I am with you. After all you have only had a few days to learn, you have achieved more in that time than some sorcerers have achieved in many years. You have a great gift, Sabella, I'm sure you will become one of my very best students. But don't get too carried away for you still have many years of work and training to catch up on. There are still powers to learn and endless books to study. That's why aboard your ship the Compton there is a full copy of not only the room we are in right now with its maps of the skies and the oceans, but also your quarters with its own library. I will also project myself in holographic form on a daily basis so I can carry on teaching you. The voyage to the ice is roughly a few weeks weather permitting; I can teach you a great deal in that time," said Marmaduke.

"Don't worry I will work as hard as I need to, to gain as much knowledge as I can before I get there," Sabella replied.

Giving her a reassuring smile Marmaduke leaned forward on his sticks and said. "The time is near, Sabella, for you to set sail on your ship and head for the ice. Tobias waits for you at the end of the corridor."

Turning, Sabella walked off down the steps and beyond the crystal pool.

"Sorceress," called Marmaduke.

"Yes?" Sabella replied turning to face him.

"Please come home safe to Castle Cove."

"I will I promise, I have to, so many people are depending on me," said Sabella giving her teacher a wave. She then walked to the end of the corridor, opened the door stepping out into the bright sunshine.

"Good morning," came a familiar voice.

Although she couldn't see him, for her eyes had not yet adjusted to the sun, she knew it was Tobias.

"Morning," Sabella answered shielding her face.

"Your ship is ready," Tobias explained. "Stocked with supplies, we set sail in half an hour, so we better go and give you a tour of the Compton and get you settled in."

Walking from the castle to the cove wall Tobias ushered her along through the market, the hordes of people wanted to wish them luck on their voyage. Eventually they stepped out from under the big stone arch and onto the sand, hearing a bang as the gate closed behind them and locked into place. As they walked over to the steps, Sabella could see the three tall masts of the Compton reaching high into the air. Climbing up the steps they stepped onto the wall, where all the hustle and bustle from the previous day had stopped and was now replaced with calmness.

Just a couple of unusual looking sea birds sat eating the remains of the fish that had been caught that morning.

The Compton, which looked bigger than ever, sat in the water, gently rolling backwards and forwards on its bow and stern lines. Walking along the wall towards it, a whistle sounded signalling their arrival. By the time they had reached the gangplank the crew had assembled in a line ready to meet her and Tobias who had turned himself into captain of the Compton, a job that he had always done being a very accomplished seaman. He knew the oceans better than anyone. Walking across the plank which had a slight uphill rise to it, Sabella stepped onto the lovely shiny black deck. In front of her stood the crew, walking over Tobias introduced each one in turn. A couple of them she already knew, one she knew very well indeed, for it was her little shiny friend and servant Jester. Standing next to him was another robot practically identical to him but this one was silver in colour.

"Hello again, Jester," Sabella smiled before turning to the robot next to him.

"Sabella, this is Paiter," Tobias explained. "He is the pilot of the Compton, might I add a very good seaman; I assure you we are in very good hands with him at the helm. He is also the brother of Jester."

"I thought I could see a resemblance between you two," Sabella said smiling which in turn made Tobias laugh. Bending down she looked at Paiter.

"I hope that once we get underway, I have some spare moments, that I can spend a little more time with you learning more about your job on the Compton if that's alright?"

"It will be a pleasure," Paiter replied in a softly spoken voice.

Moving along the line, she said hello to the dooadite twins, Kaylum and Keltal, who she already knew. Then onto the very strange fellow at the end who was quite tall, also thin as a stick. In fact he was so thin that all of his features seemed oversized. His nose, ears and eyes all looked like they belonged to someone else. Even his hair and eyebrows which were light grey in colour were big and bushy. He was acting very nervous and was moving about like he couldn't stand still for a single second.

"This is Professor Brumbles," Tobias explained. "He is responsible for all mechanical things in Castle Cove like the

Compton, the twins, Jester and Paiter. They were all made by him."

"Hello, Professor," said Sabella extending her hand towards him which he quickly grabbed hold of and shook quite hard.

"Hello, Sorceress, I am very pleased to meet you finally," he said in a very high-pitched voice like he was on helium.

"I have heard a lot about you, Professor Brumbles; just like the others I would like to spend some time with you. I have a great deal to learn while we sail to the ice and your wealth of knowledge is something I can learn from," Sabella said.

"It will be a great honour," the Professor squeaked, shaking her hand a little faster and tighter before letting go.

"Listen up everyone," ordered Tobias. "If you will all go to your stations, we will make ready to sail. Remember time and tide wait for no man."

"Tobias where are the rest of the crew? Are there more down below?" Sabella asked.

"No," Tobias laughed. "The Compton doesn't need a crew. Professor Brumbles has built it in such a way that everything is controlled by Paiter up in the wheelhouse. I will be happy to show you around once we have set sail," Tobias replied before looking up at the wheelhouse. "Are you ready, Paiter?"

"Yes, Captain," replied the little robot.

Kaylum and Keltal, who had gone to either end of the ship, got the signal from Tobias and cast off their bow and stern lines. Powering up the engine, big paddles on either side of the ship started to turn. The water bubbled and boiled as the huge ship slowly started to come away from the wall.

"All clear," came a shout from the twins.

"Thank you," replied Tobias who once again looked up to the wheelhouse. "All clear, Paiter, bring her round, full steam ahead if you please."

"Will do, Captain," Paiter replied.

With the bow lined up to the horizon, Paiter put the Compton on full power. Slowly picking up speed the ship pulled away from the castle wall and settled into a steady rhythm. With the sound of the paddles gaining speed they left a long trail of churned up water behind them. It wasn't long before the castle was just a little dot in the distance, eventually disappearing completely leaving them alone on a crystal blue, calm sea.

Sabella stared into the distance to where Castle Cove lay beyond the horizon. She felt a little sadness as she was just starting to settle into life in the castle as a sorceress, and now she was going many miles away from not only her new home but the doorway to her old one as well. It was going to be a long time before she returned but at least she had her friends on board with her.

"Would you like a tour of the ship now?" Tobias asked.

"Yes please," Sabella said turning to face him smiling.

"We will start up here first then," Tobias explained. "The Compton is one hundred and fifty meters long and can move at thirty knots. She can run by her engine or by sail if the wind is in our favour. As you can see there isn't a lot on deck apart from the wheelhouse and the door leading down to the lower decks. The reason for that is if we get attacked during the night then firstly, nothing will get damaged and secondly we can put the shields up," Tobias said pointing to a groove that ran around the whole perimeter of the ship.

"How high do they come up?" Sabella asked.

"They don't really come up but over. They cover the whole ship completely just leaving the three masts protruding above. At some point during our journey to the ice, the shields will have to go up," Tobias said seeing the shocked look upon her face. "But rest assured the Compton is very safe. Now let's go below and I will show you the rest of the ship."

Walking across the deck to a door, Tobias opened it and they stepped in. With the door shut behind them there was silence, not a sound. Moments before, there had been the sound of the churning water and the noise of the paddles but now it didn't even feel like a ship. Walking down a steep set of steps they ended up in a long corridor which ran from one end of the ship to the other. Brightly coloured pillars ran down both walls and each one was a different colour to the next.

"This corridor, Sabella, is the heart of the ship and as you can see it too is made up of pillars. Each one being made up of a different stone," said Tobias.

Reaching out and running her hand down the smooth glass finish of one of them. "The floor is so beautiful," Sabella said, referring to the crystal blue marble tiles inlayed with yet more symbols and lit by a continuous line of light that ran down the side of either wall.

"Let's go this way first," Tobias pointed as they started to walk down the beautiful corridor. As they went on Tobias was explaining to her what went on behind each of the doors but she wasn't really listening. Her mind was fascinated by the corridor and all its pillars; she couldn't help wondering how they came to be on the Compton, as it was an old looking ship. There was something undiscovered about all this, for some reason it was playing on her mind. She didn't know why but it was intriguing her enough to probe a little deeper.

Tobias stopped at a door, looking up Sabella saw the sign reading 'Engine Room'.

"Do you want to see the engine room?" Tobias asked, "I must confess although I'm the captain I know nothing about how all this works. I tend to leave all that to the Professor as he is the expert. It's far too technical for me but it's amazing to look at."

"Okay," Sabella nodded, "I would like to see it if I may."

Tobias opened the door and they stepped through onto a small metal landing. In front of them was a long set of iron tread steps which led down deep into the ship. Although she couldn't see the engine, she could hear it. It wasn't loud; it was more like someone using a sink plunger with a kind of squelching sound. At the foot of the steps, multi-coloured lights like a rainbow shone off the walls. As they made their way further down, the engine came into view, standing some ten meters tall. It looked like a very old steam engine with its four big pistons moving backwards and forwards into the cylinders. But this engine was different for there was no dirty coal or hot smoky boilers. No oil splattered everywhere or big lumps of grease hanging off. This one was spotlessly clean; the cylinders were made of glass, so you could see the pistons moving in and out of them. Clear pipes led from each cylinder head, off around the wall to eight glass jars. Each one about two meters tall filled with a coloured liquid. As the piston went down, it sucked in a small amount from each jar where they were mixed. A chemical reaction took place where they exploded in the colours of the rainbow. Each piston did this simultaneously powering the ship forward.

"What do you think?" Tobias asked.

"It's amazing, did the Professor make all of this on his own?" said Sabella in awe.

"I guess he did," replied Tobias, looking puzzled at her question. "But then again I have never asked him; he just turned up with it one day. He's ingenious and has made some fantastic things in the past. Why have you got concerns about him?" Tobias asked.

"No, not at all," Sabella replied trying to put his mind at rest but deep down she did have questions. Something in the back of her mind was questioning the Professor's credibility. He may have well-built Jester and Paiter and helped the twins, he probably was a very clever man, but this engine seemed far more advanced than the abilities of one man. Maybe she was being sceptical, undermining the brilliance of the Professor. Maybe when she spent some time with him it would put her mind at rest but only time would tell.

Climbing back up the stairs Tobias closed the door to the engine room and they stood in silence once more. Carrying on along the corridor they came to a stop outside another door with a sign over it reading, 'Laboratory'.

"This is the Professor's room, from here he keeps the Compton running smoothly, making sure the robots are working properly. Unfortunately, that little red light up there," Tobias said pointing above the door, "means he is busy right now and doesn't want to be disturbed. But you can come back later if you like."

"I will as it will be good to talk to him about his work and I am very interested in what he has to tell me."

"Rather you than me," Tobias said laughing. "When he gets talking there is no stopping him. He often sends me to sleep with his warbling about electric circuitry, power surges and other useless information but if that's what you want to know he is more than happy to talk about it."

Tobias carried on down the corridor until they could go no further, stopping outside the last door. "These are your quarters, my room is just over there," he said pointing. "So, I am very close if you need me. I will leave you now to have a look around and I will meet you up on deck in a while, for once we get far enough out to sea and the wind picks up, we will be setting the sails."

"Alright then, I will just have a quick look and will then come straight up," Sabella replied.

With Tobias making his way down the pillared corridor and back up the steps which led up to the main deck, Sabella opened the door to her quarters stepping in. Standing in a small passageway, looking around it was luxury like she had never seen before as everything was highly polished marble, the walls were as black as night and shiny like mirrors. Walking forward into the main living quarters the lights came on automatically. In front of her was the biggest bed she could have imagined, what was even better was it was round in shape, but still there was something even more impressive.

All the fixtures and fittings were made of what looked like precious metals. Gold, silver, even platinum adorned every part of the room. The chairs, table, even her cutlery which Jester had already laid out for her was polished silver. Just off of this room was her bathroom, she peered around the door into it. Once again this room was filled with even more gold and silver. The bath itself looked like it had been carved from a solid block of gold, she couldn't wait to try it out.

Moving on down the small passageway, the lights turned on and off as she now entered a room which appeared as the library, she recognised some of the books on the shelves. The sweetest thing for Sabella was that Jester had laid a book out on the carved gold table, it was the last book she had been reading back at the castle. He had kindly opened it up to the page she had read up to.

At the back of the room was a set of double doors engraved with more writing and symbols which were gleaming. She made her way over to them and took hold of the handles, there was a loud click and she pushed them open. The light came on and revealed a triangular shaped room, like the corridor outside it too was lined with pillars. In the centre of the room sat a crystal pool, it also had the maps of the seas and stars like the ones in the castle on the floor and ceiling. Maybe, this was the training room where Marmaduke was going to teach her during the voyage, she thought to herself.

Just then there was a whistle from the other room which made her jump and spin around. She left the room, went to investigate where the noise had come from, soon finding that it was coming from a talk tube which was hanging from the wall.

Picking it up, she pulled out the stopper and spoke, "Hello, Sabella here."

"It's Tobias we are just about to set the sails. Are you coming up?"

"I'm on my way," Sabella replied placing the talk tube back on the wall and leaving her quarters to walk along the pillar lined corridor to the steps. Climbing up them she opened the door at the top, it was very odd going from total silence to hearing the outside noise once more. Also now they were in open water with no sign of land and the wind had now picked up.

"Sabella, over here," Tobias called.

Walking over towards him, she looked at the masts towering high above her and suddenly thought how strange it was that they didn't have any ropes on them. She couldn't even see any sails which were normally tied up at the top on sailing ships. Then again this was no normal ship so she decided to watch first and ask questions later. Standing next to Tobias who was stood in front of the wheelhouse she watched him turn to look up at Paiter and call. "Bring her round into the wind, set the sails and head due north if you please."

"Alright, Captain," came the reply.

Slowly, the Compton turned, listing slightly to port as the bow swung around to face north.

"Setting the sails," yelled Paiter.

Looking up at the masts, Sabella saw that they had slowly started to turn and there was a clicking sound, all of a sudden the masts slowly opened up like giant fans. The effect of this was so great that the ship leapt forward and immediately gained speed. So much so that it made her unsteady on her feet and she had to step backwards to regain her footing.

"What do you think?" shouted Tobias over the noise of the wind rushing against the sails.

"It's amazing and so fast," she shouted back.

"Come with me," Tobias called to her.

Making their way forward to the bow Sabella grabbed hold of the railing which ran around the deck of the ship. The feeling of speed was multiplied as she looked down at the bow of the Compton cutting its way through the waves, causing each one to explode down the side of the ship in big white clouds of mist. Looking towards the horizon with sea spray on their face and the taste of salt on their lips they sailed on to the unknown. The island of ice.

Chapter 9

A few days had passed by and Sabella pushed open the doors to her training room ready for her morning's lesson with Marmaduke. The ship had settled into a routine, they were making good time as the weather was still in their favour, bright sunshine with clear blue skies and a steady breeze.

She had spent time with the dooadite twins scrubbing the decks and polishing the tons of brass and copper which adorned the deck of the Compton. Sabella had learnt what many of the hundreds of buttons were for in the wheelhouse with Paiter. Spending many evenings eating with Tobias, Sabella listened to all his knowledge on maps, oceans, weather patterns, rip tides and under currents before returning to her quarters for more studying, this time on the enemy. Each night she had started to study in detail one of her three evil adversaries, the chameleon warrior, the viper warrior and the bearded dragon warrior.

Over the next few weeks, Sabella hoped to gain an in-depth knowledge of all three. There was obviously one more being, Mortigan himself but there was no knowledge of him in any books, leaving only the teachings of Marmaduke to go on. She still hoped that he was safely locked up under the ice and that all of this had been for nothing. But something told her deep down it was going to be far from easy, not knowing why or for what reason the dreams that she had been having would be connected in some way. They were more like flashes in her thoughts seeing herself standing in the castle looking out across the sea at a big black wave coming towards her. It was always the same dream that came to her.

A faint shimmer at the end of the room told her that Marmaduke was on his way, slowly an image started to appear. It was so life like that you could have mistaken it to be a real person.

"Good Morning, Sabella, I take it you are well today?" said Marmaduke.

"Very well thank you," Sabella replied.

"Good, good, because from today onwards we step-up your training. So please stand in front of the pool." Marmaduke had no time to waste.

Walking over, she did as he asked.

"Now shut your eyes and relax, for what I want you to do now is slowly turn your body but keep your feet still," Marmaduke ordered. "Just your top half, now let your arms hang loose and turn slowly to the left, followed by the right keeping in time with the fountain."

It took a long time but suddenly the core of her stomach felt butterflies, slowly spreading around her whole body making her hands and feet feel red hot with pins and needles, giving her the strength and the feeling of enormous power.

"Now, Sabella, call the fire army," her teacher ordered. "But keep moving, don't lose concentration."

Remembering her long nights of studying she spoke the words of the fire orb. "Army of fire reignite,

"Rise up from your fishers,

"Prepare to fight."

"Again keep going," Marmaduke said with haste.

As she repeated it over and over again a strange noise entered the room. A roaring sound echoed around accompanied by cracking and popping that was appearing to get louder.

"Now very slowly open your eyes," her teacher said, "Do not panic, remember you are safe, for what you are seeing is just a trick of the mind."

Doing as her teacher asked, she opened her eyes, instantly she felt her heart beating like a drum on her chest. Her breathing became more rapid, she gasped in short sharp breaths to try to calm herself down. For in front of her, now stood a fire warrior where just a few moments ago the crystal blue pool and fountain was in its place. She could clearly see a human shape amongst the yellow, orange and red flames, but it appeared more like a ghost or even a shadow. With no distinguishing features, just dark holes showed themselves where the eyes and mouth were supposed to be. Flames had also spread out over the sides of the pool, they were creeping across the floor and up the walls like a plague of insects. Eventually they moved across the ceiling so that the whole room was covered in a blanket of fire.

"Sabella, stop turning," ordered Marmaduke shouting above all the noise.

Doing as he asked, she brought her hands to rest at her sides and stopped turning. Suddenly, there was a very loud noise like someone had turned on a giant vacuum cleaner and the flames were sucked back from across the ceiling, back down the walls and across the floor into the pool. Taking with it the fire warrior who disappeared into a giant puff of smoke, leaving the room back to normal with the crystal blue pool and fountain once again in the middle.

Falling to her knees, Sabella gasped for air.

"Are you alright, Sabella?" Marmaduke asked.

"Just feeling very tired, what's happening to me?" Sabella questioned almost quivering at the experience.

"That's normal and it will get better with practice. You have just completed four hours of training."

"Four hours?" she said, shocked. "It only felt like ten minutes, no wonder I'm worn out." Catching her breath, she turned to face Marmaduke. "So that was a fire warrior?"

"Yes, indeed it was, and if you had the fire orb, which you don't for it is with your mother, then you could summon the army. Like all the orbs, if you are in possession of it you can use it, making you very powerful indeed."

"Can I ask you a question please?" Sabella said.

"Of course you can. I'm always here to answer anything you would like to know," Marmaduke trying to reassure her.

"Why are the orbs here on this planet and not on Earth where they were?" Sabella asked with so many worries.

"That is a very good question, Sabella, but one you shouldn't be worrying about now, you should be concentrating on the task at hand. However, seeing as you have asked, I will explain. A thousand years ago, Castle Cove that you know was identical to this one, peaceful, safe and tranquil. Until the day Mortigan found out where the orbs were hidden. You see when you look into the sky at night, you see hundreds of thousands of stars and among them there are planets similar to this one. Of course as you know Earth is one of them and was one of the better ones being hidden deep in the outer reaches of space.

One of Mortigan's many armies however managed to track the orbs down. Coming down from the heavens, they threatened to destroy Earth and its people, destroying the castle in the initial battle. So the decision was taken to move the orbs to a new planet, hence why they are now here on Knighton."

"So when did Mortigan find them here?" Sabella asked. "From the very start I'm afraid, he discovered where the orbs were going and followed them. A great battle then took place eventually ending with Mortigan being banished to his icy tomb by the sorceress at the time who sacrificed her life for the orbs. Still up till now no one else has ever fought the evil one," Marmaduke replied.

"So why haven't the orbs been moved to a new planet? Surely it would be a great opportunity to do this while he's imprisoned?"

"You are right it would be but in the battle many key and important people were killed sadly along with my father, with them the knowledge on how to move the orbs," Marmaduke sighed, "The people who did survive passed on the knowledge that they had, I took over the training of the future sorceress and the skills they would need to protect the orbs."

"So you're saying they can never be moved?" said Sabella.

"I'm afraid so, they can only ever be moved and hidden on Knighton and only by you, they are far too powerful, only someone with a heart of pure love or evil can hold or move them. But there is no way of knowing that for certain until we eventually get to one. We don't possess the knowledge or know how to move them to a different planet. All has sadly been lost, as I was too young to be passed the many secrets," Marmaduke answered appearing very gloomy.

"One thing is nagging me which I find odd, if we don't know how to move them off Knighton how did my mother the Sorceress managed to carry one through the portal door in a metal and wooden box. Why can't we find the remaining orbs and do the same?" asked Sabella.

"I and the Professor did look into it; it appears that the box is made of a magic metal not found on Knighton. If we had more boxes it would make it easy to move them but we don't," grumbled Marmaduke.

Sabella thought for a moment, things were not adding up; there were many unanswered questions to be answered if she were to protect the orbs from evil.

"So what are the symbols and pillars?" Sabella questioned.

"Again all those who knew the true meanings perished and we have no way of deciphering them."

"But if Mortigan has been entombed for a thousand years under the ice, why or how would he escape after so long?" asked Sabella.

"He has tried many times in the past to escape but all were unsuccessful. That's why we must check on him this time and make sure he is still safely imprisoned," said Marmaduke.

"Just one more thing. What of his army? Where are they?" Sabella had so many questions.

"In the wide expanse of oceans, Sabella. There are many places to hide, they do attack occasionally but always unsuccessfully. They are killers and barbarians but they need leadership in order to mount a substantial attack. So while Mortigan is under the ice, we and the orbs are safe," said Marmaduke.

"It's all still a bit confusing but in time I'm sure I will make sense of it all," said Sabella, reassuring herself.

"It will come good in time, I suggest you rest for a few hours before studying some more," Marmaduke advised her.

"I think you're right," she replied, "I do feel very tired, I will see you tomorrow."

The hologram of Marmaduke disappeared and Sabella returned to her quarters. She climbed into bed and was soon fast asleep.

Chapter 10

With a loud scream Sabella opened her eyes and looked up at the ceiling, for a second or two she had no idea where she was. Rubbing her eyes, she gathered her senses, why was she having these dreams about a big black wave that was heading towards the castle. Staring up she listened intently for any noise in her eerily quiet room, no noise at all, however Sabella had a strong sense of smell. Looking to her right a plate sat on the side covered with a lid, sitting up and swinging her legs over the side of the bed she lifted the lid to find a huge plate of chicken and chips. Having not eaten at all that day she couldn't eat it fast enough, enjoying every mouthful.

With the last chip disappearing into her mouth, she glanced over at her clock which read 'eleven o'clock pm'. She had been asleep nearly all day, obviously needing it. Jumping off the bed she walked into the study room and sat at her desk, flicking through a very old book with lovely illustrated pictures of Castle Cove and its surrounding island. There were maps and sketches of where to find the best fauna and flora for particular medicines and potions.

Maybe when they returned from the voyage and all was well again with her mother back through the door, she could spend some time exploring her new home and all it had to offer. But at the moment that all seemed a long way off, Sabella just hoped it wasn't too long.

Closing the book as her mind began to wander to other things, she thought some fresh air might do her some good after being asleep all day. Shutting the door behind her she looked over to the room belonging to Tobias, but thought better than knocking in case she woke him. Walking along the pillared corridor she stopped at the Professor's door. Maybe this would be a good time to catch up with him as she hadn't seen him since the first day on deck at the start of their voyage. Tapping the door, she put her ear against it and listened. A rustling sound could be heard followed by quick footsteps which told her the Professor was up and coming to answer it.

"Hello, Sabella," Professor Brumbles squeaked as he opened it.

"Hi, Professor, I see that you are still up, would it be okay to come in?" said Sabella.

"Of course it would," Professor Brumbles replied standing aside, "Please come in."

Walking into the Professor's quarters she was immediately hit with how it looked. It was nothing like her room at all, it appeared to be full of junk; bits of metal, cables and circuitry lay everywhere. Some circuit boards were hooked up to monitors that flickered with wavy lines.

"Do you mind if I just finish something quickly?" The Professor asked.

"Of course not, please carry on," Sabella replied taking great interest in her surroundings. Walking towards the back of the room she looked at rows of jars sat upon shelves. Each one filled with specimens of creatures, and whatever liquid they were stored in had turned them a white colour as if they were made of wax. Glancing along she passed a strange contraption sat on a workbench, made of hundreds of glass tubes; all carrying different coloured substances, like the engine room but much smaller. Back and forward the coloured liquid moved before dripping into conical flasks where it bubbled and boiled.

Turning around, she looked at the Professor who had his head down working on a piece of electrical equipment. She watched as he welded bits together, little puffs of smoke rose into the air. To her right sat the Professor's desk, she couldn't see much of it as it was virtually covered in rubbish from paper and charts, to equipment and tools. But one thing in particular did catch her eye, in the middle something big and round sat underneath a sheet. It looked about twice the size of a football. Walking over she took hold of one corner of the cover and lifted it up.

"Please be careful with that," came a voice from behind her making her jump.

"Oh sorry, Professor, I was just looking." Sabella sounding startled.

"That's alright, Sabella," the Professor said, "You need to see it."

Reaching forward he took hold of the sheet and pulled it off. There sat in the middle of the desk was a round silver ball with a copper coloured band running around the middle, containing little coloured lights. On top was an indentation with a red button in the middle

"This, Sabella, is my freeze bomb. It has taken me many years to perfect, harness and control the power needed to make it work properly," explained the Professor.

"So, what's it used for, Professor?" she asked.

"You, Sabella, will be taking it across the ice with you. When you get there, you will set it to go off," the Professor explained.

"Then what happens?" she quizzed.

"Once you have pressed this," he said pointing to the red button on the top, "there is no stopping it. You have one hour to get as far away as possible," said the Professor.

"Now I'm a little worried, please go on," insisted Sabella rather impatiently.

"At the pressing of the button the freeze bomb becomes red hot and as it melts down through the ice it will gain speed. Once the hour is up it will detonate and freeze everything dead or alive on, in or under Stenbury," answered the Professor.

"Oh I see," Sabella said, "But correct me if I'm wrong, I think we will still be out there on the ice when it goes off. Are you sure you have thought of everything?"

"Yes, yes I have," he squealed waving his arms around, "come this way."

Walking over to another part of the room and bending down he picked up a rucksack, opened it and reached in. He pulled out something that looked like a rolled up sleeping bag. Untying the string and holding it together, the Professor threw it out in front of him, instantly as if by magic it popped up into a triangle shaped tent.

"This, Sabella, is your protection from the freeze bomb. It's made of a special material that I designed myself. It will hopefully withstand the explosion's freeze."

"You say hopefully, Professor, have you actually tested it against the freeze bomb? Is it a tent?" Sabella's voice almost quivering.

"Well not as such," the Professor replied sheepishly. "But it worked well here under laboratory conditions."

"So it's not been tested really?" Sabella quizzed. "Come to think of it, what about the bomb itself? Please tell me this is not the first one you have ever made?"

The Professor turned and put his hand on the silver ball.

"Professor," Sabella asked again raising her voice, "Is this the first bomb you have ever made?"

"Yes," he replied turning back to face her, "It will be alright as I have calculated everything. It will work perfectly I assure you."

"I hope you're right, Professor, as a lot depends on us making it back safely and in one piece. While we are on the subject of making it home, I would like to speak to you about the Compton, and its amazing engine room," said Sabella.

"What about the engine room?" the Professor mumbled as he turned and walked across the room.

"Well I would like to know some more about it, and how you built it."

"Well maybe not now, it's getting very late," he replied, "Can we leave it for another day?" The Professor added quickly putting on a set of goggles and picking up a soldering iron he carried on working.

"Maybe another time then," Sabella said sensing that he had just made an excuse to get out of talking about it, which just reignited her earlier concerns about everything. He was a very clever man, whose heart was in the right place, but the engine was another matter, it was a missing piece to the puzzle that she had to find the answer to.

"I will see you again soon, Professor," Sabella called as she headed for the door. Keeping his head down, the Professor lifted his hand and waved as she stepped out the door, closing it behind her.

Looking up the corridor, the pillars were lit by two thin rows of lights; it always felt as though Sabella was on two ships, as there was such a contrast between the corridor which was made of stone and the upper decks with its thick plated metal. Maybe the Professor would be easier to talk to when he wasn't so busy. He had to tell her about the engine at some point, he couldn't hide it forever. Maybe on the way home was the best time, for as they neared Stenbury she could sense everyone getting a little more nervous.

Still wide awake, she looked at her watch and saw that it was now ten minutes till midnight. She decided that she could do with some fresh air and headed towards the steps, climbed up and stepped through the door at the top into the cool night's air. The Compton had slowed considerably due to lack of wind, the sails were still up but the ship was now being powered by its engine, gently pushing itself through the calm, flat sea.

Walking past the wheelhouse, she looked up to wave to Paiter but he was busy, Sabella could only see the top of his head. Carrying on to the stern she sat down, looking up at the bright night sky. Many thousands of bright lights shone back at her, including Knighton's four moons which looked bigger than ever against the black sky.

While she was on deck, Jester had gone to her quarters to check on her as she had been asleep all day. Walking into her room he was surprised not to see her in bed. Looking around he quickly realised she wasn't there. Walking over to the talk tube he picked it up and called Tobias, just to check that she was safe with him.

"Hello, Tobias," came a sleepy voice on the other end.

"Sir its Jester, I'm in Sabella's quarters and she's not here. I take it she's not with you either?"

"No, I was sound asleep. Maybe she is with the Professor; I know she was keen to talk to him. It's probably a case of they have both lost track of time, you know how the Professor can talk. I will pop across just to check, thank you for letting me know Jester," Tobias said, hanging up before getting dressed he proceeded out of his quarters over to the Professor's room. Tapping on his door, not waiting for a reply, he turned the handle and walked straight in.

"Professor, it's Tobias; is Sabella here with you?"

"No, Captain," he replied looking up from his work. "Sabella was here a little while back. I assumed that she had gone back to her quarters."

Tobias looked at his watch and saw that it was nearly midnight. "Damn it," he said under his breath, "Professor call Paiter, tell him to keep an eye out for her. I'm going to look for her." Turning, he ran out of the door, up the pillared corridor, and up the steps bursting out through the door at the top onto the deck. First looking towards the bow then the stern, he couldn't see her anywhere. "Paiter," Tobias shouted, "Have you seen Sabella?"

"Yes, Captain, she is safe and sitting behind the wheelhouse."

Putting his hands over his face Tobias let out a sigh of relief and started walking to the stern of the ship. Seeing him approach she called out, "Tobias, over here."

"What are you doing out here? Why didn't you let anyone know where you were?" Tobias asked in stern voice.

"I didn't want to disturb you. I couldn't sleep, it's amazing up here just look at that sky."

"Sabella, please look at me, this is very serious."

"What is it?" Sabella asked realising he was a bit agitated.

"Listen you must always tell me when you come up on deck as it's my job to keep you as safe as possible. Please from now on always inform me, especially at night. Have you any idea of the time?" said Tobias.

"Yes," she replied, "It must be close to twelve, which is the time for the dead of night, I also know that we are not over a deep-sea ridge yet, so I'm perfectly safe yes?"

"Wrong you are never safe during the dead of night for this is the time when the sky is at its darkest. It only takes one small cloud to appear in the right place and make it dark enough for a viper warrior to get on board and in an instant you are dead. Do you understand me, Sabella?"

"Sorry, Tobias," she answered.

"That's okay no harm has been done. I'm just relieved you are safe, now come with me." Walking over to the side of the ship, he turned to face her. "Now, Sabella, we are in shallow water meaning that very small amounts of light can penetrate to the bottom. This makes it very hard for the warriors to get up to the surface and on board. If we were over deeper water, they would follow the light up as it gets darker making it much easier to launch an attack. Many hundreds die every night coming up to the surface but that doesn't stop them from trying."

"So, you're saying that there are viper warriors under the boat now?" Sabella was trying to keep calm.

Looking at his watch Tobias turned to the wheelhouse and gave a nod to Paiter who flicked two switches. Firstly, a fluorescent blue light shone out below the water line under the ship, and secondly a very strong ring of sunlight, like an inch-wide laser beam, ran around the ship halfway down the hull. So bright was this light that it shone far into the distance. Tobias turned and looked over the side, "Look," he said.

Carefully, taking hold of the railings she peered over the side. There swimming alongside of the ship were lots of viperfish, not being affected by the special fluorescent light at all.

"It's now the dead of night, Sabella," Tobias explained, "Once they see us this happens."

Right on queue they were spotted and some of the viperfish took their chance to make their attack, as they leapt from the water. Each one changing from a fish to a warrior as they left the sea. In mid-flight they drew their weapons and with mouths open making gurgling roars they hit the sunlight beam and instantly vaporised into a ghostly cloud of dust. Time and time again this happened until the dead of night had passed. Then as quickly as they had appeared the evil army sunk back into the black abyss below.

"Now do you see why I need you to tell me where you are?" Tobias asked.

"Yes, I'm very sorry Tobias it won't happen again."

"In the morning we will be heading away from the shallows into deep sea for the next few days and the weather doesn't look good, get some rest," Tobias said.

"Alright then I will see you in the morning, goodnight." Walking across the deck, down the steps and along the corridor to her quarters Sabella realised she still had a lot to learn if she was ever going to survive this journey.

Chapter 11

Feeling a little queasy, Sabella had got out of bed early due to the Compton rolling from side to side, in ever worsening seas. It made training with Marmaduke very interesting, and although she shouldn't have laughed, she couldn't help herself watching Jester wobbling around like a drunken robot.

Leaving her quarters, she put her arms out, holding onto the pillars to help steady herself as she made her way across to Tobias' quarters. Tapping the door, she heard a familiar deep shout to come in. Stepping in she staggered across to the table, with Tobias laughing loudly at her unsteady sea legs.

"It's not funny," Sabella said grabbing hold of the table and sitting down. She was trying so hard to keep a straight face, but seeing Tobias laughing his head off she soon cracked before they both fell about in fits of laughter. Calming themselves down they got on with the more serious task in hand which was making it across one of the deepest sea ridges on Knighton. Unrolling a large map on the table, Sabella held onto it whilst Tobias placed large weights on each corner to hold it down, and to stop it from rolling back up.

"Right, Sabella, we are here at the moment," pointed Tobias, "In the next hour we will be leaving shallow waters and heading across a deep ridge. We need to cross it as fast as possible but the weather is very much against us."

"How bad is it going to get?" Sabella asked.

"It's going to be pretty nasty, we will have to bring down the sails and go on engine power alone. I am hoping that it will only be two days and one night but the way the weather looks we might not make it across to here," Tobias said pointing again at the map. "So, at the moment we have everything against us, but the Compton is an amazing ship, she will get us there I'm sure of it."

"I won't deny it," Sabella confessed, "I am a little scared, not only by the sea and the weather, but also being attacked from below by Mortigan's army."

"It's good to be a little scared, Sabella, it keeps us all on our toes, I am a little nervous myself but let's hope the weather calms down and we make it across in two days." Rolling up the map he stood up. "Why don't you come up on deck for some fresh air? For once we get out of the shallow waters, I will need you to stay down below for your own safety."

Making their way carefully down the corridor they climbed the steps, opened the door and stepped out onto the deck. The wind had definitely picked up and was whirling around the ship making whistling sounds as it went past the sails.

"Sabella," shouted Tobias. "Please stand in front of the wheelhouse and hold on, don't move unless I tell you too."

"Okay," she shouted back.

Keltal and Kaylum had also joined them on deck, they were checking that everything was safely fastened and secured down in preparation for the storm ahead. It was quite thrilling as the wind rushed around her, a fine mist of sea spray hanging in the air as the ship pitched from side to side cutting its way through the waves. Suddenly, the excitement stopped when she looked out onto the horizon, for they were sailing into a wall of water. Giant waves with white tops could clearly be seen as they moved ever closer to the edge of the deep ridge. Thick black angry clouds were building overhead, thunder and lightning could be heard and seen in the distance.

Standing in front of her Tobias looked up at the wheelhouse. "Retract the sails please Paiter," he shouted.

"Will do, Captain," came the reply of Paiter.

There was a loud clicking sound before the masts starting turning, drawing the massive metal sails back in, reducing the pace of the Compton back down to a crawl.

"All safely in, Captain," came a voice from above.

"Thank you," Tobias replied, "Kaylum and Keltal is everything water tight on deck?"

"Yes, Captain," they chorused.

"Then please go below and make sure the Professor is alright and ready."

As the twins headed off Tobias turned and looked at Sabella who was transfixed by the angry boiling mass of water that lay in front of them.

"Sabella," came a voice. "It's time to get you downstairs," said Tobias breaking her train of thought.

"Sorry I was just thinking," Sabella said.

"We must be quick now," Tobias beckoned her and together they walked towards the door. He helped her inside before taking a long hard look at the storm ahead. He then stepped inside himself and turned to look up at Paiter.

"Take care, my little friend."

Shutting the door, he had one last look out of the window before turning and hanging onto the railings as they descended the stairs and went along the corridor with the ship rolling and pitching a little more. Standing outside her door, Tobias turned to face Sabella.

"Now I need you to stay in your room. Jester has been in there and has tried to make everything safe but things are still going to move around so please be careful. I will call on you from time to time to check you're alright as its going to be a tough day or two, you probably won't get much sleep. We will be alright though I can assure you."

Not wanting to show how scared she really was, Sabella said her goodbyes to Tobias and stepped in through her door closing it behind her. Instantly, she slid to the floor and burst into tears. Although she trusted Tobias with her life, this was the first time she had to deal with anything this frightening on her own without her mother, but she knew that somehow she had to get through it and be strong. Wiping her eyes and getting back on her feet, she held onto the wall and walked into the main room of her quarters.

Feeling very alone and helpless, she wobbled into her library and sat down at her desk where she opened a book. Flicking through the pages, Sabella tried to take her mind off of the oncoming storm. Looking down, she realised that her chair had been fixed to the floor, along with the table and various other items around her quarters, from books to ornaments, all which had either been packed away or secured down which was a good job, as suddenly the ship's bow started to climb. Higher and higher it went until her chair was virtually on its side. There was a slight pause as the ship crested the wave, slowly like a seesaw at first but then gaining speed the bow started to drop and dive down into the trough of the wave sending her stomach into her mouth. Scared stiff she clung onto the chair with her knuckles turning white as she tried to stop herself from being thrown across the room. As the ship went into what felt like a vertical dive, she let out a scream. Down it went until a shudder rippled through the Compton signalling as it had reached the bottom of the wave before the bow started to slowly rise up the next wave face.

After an hour or more of sheer panic, wondering if the ship was ever going to make it over the next wave Sabella had another problem. She was losing the feeling in her hands and arms from holding on so tightly, her legs were becoming bruised and sore. She didn't know how much longer she could last as the pain in them was becoming unbearable, her muscles were burning. Thinking fast, she had a plan that at the bottom of the next wave she was going to make a run for it, for as the ship settled in each trough, she had counted a three-second gap where it was reasonably steady and flat. That was all the time she had to make it to her bed, jump on and hold on tight. Her arms and legs were hurting so much; it had to be on this wave. So as the ship shuddered to a stop she took off, running around her desk down the hallway, counting the seconds as she went, *one, two, three,* the ship started moving once more.

So powerful was the movement of the floor as it climbed the next wave that her legs buckled diving forwards. As she fell, she grabbed hold of her bed, hanging on as the ship violently climbed. By the crest of the wave, her legs were hanging in mid-air. As it pivoted over the top once more, she climbed onto the bed where she grabbed her pillow and bed cover making a dash for it once more, this time heading for her bathroom where she quickly climbed into her bath and wrapped herself up in her blanket. The sides of the bath held her in tightly, eventually after four more hours of feeling like she was on a scary roller coaster ride she fell asleep exhausted.

"Sabella, where are you?" shouted Tobias.

"In here," she called back sleepily.

Sticking his head around the door he smiled broadly, "I see you came up with a good idea."

"I didn't have a choice, how bad was it out there?" Sabella asked.

"A lot worse than we thought as we have quite a lot of damage but we made it," Tobias said reaching out a hand and helping her out of the bath.

"What kind of damage?" she enquired.

"I'm not sure as we are just assessing it all," said Tobias.

Walking from her bathroom she looked around and noticed a few books and objects scattered on the floor which wasn't much considering how violent the storm was. However, as they made their way up onto the deck the damage up there was a lot worse. She looked at the wheelhouse and saw that all of the windows had been broken and part of the roof had been ripped off. Keltal was doing his best to patch it up while Kaylum was busy repairing the railings around the ship as some had been completely torn away. Apart from that it looked like the Compton had fared well in the mountainous seas, even Paiter had survived with only a few scars. He had done an amazing job steering them through the storm, he was now busy giving Tobias a full run down on the ship's condition.

Looking out across the sea, Sabella could see that the waves had now died down. There were still black clouds rolling across the sky, she realised that it had now got much colder as they sailed further north towards the ice. Seeing Tobias walking over towards her, she noticed he had a very worried look on his face.

"Is everything alright?" Sabella asked.

"Not really, Sabella, we have a major problem." Tobias sounding concerned.

"Whatever is the matter? We're not sinking, are we?" She asked starting to worry.

"No, we are not sinking," Tobias assured her.

"But we did sustain more damage than we thought. Paiter has just informed me that the storm has knocked out the ship's defence system which means we have only a day to fix them and get them back up and running as it looks like we are possibly going to have another night over the deep-sea ridge. If we can't then we are open to attack from below as we are still over the top of it. But let's not panic as the Professor is working very hard down below, Paiter is doing his best up here so it should all be fixed by the dead of night. Anyway you better get yourself back down below as you have training and study time to catch up on."

"Are you sure I can't help?" Sabella asked.

"We will sort it so don't worry," Tobias replied, "I will come down and see you later and keep you informed. Now don't be late for Marmaduke."

Walking back to the door she stepped back inside and closed it behind her, leaving the Compton's crew to get the security system operational by nightfall.

Chapter 12

After the terrors during the night before, Sabella thought this day had gone well with a good training session from Marmaduke followed by an interesting chat afterwards which rolled on for hours. A whole range of subjects were covered from the previous night's storm, to Knighton, Castle Cove and life on the distant planet. This was followed by a good soak in the bath with more studying before spending a little time with Jester as she had barely spent any time with him since they had set sail on their voyage. He stood at the end of the bed and chatted away to her as she got stuck into a big bowl of beef stew which had appeared as if by magic in her hands, enjoying every mouthful until the bowl was empty.

With evening approaching she had not heard a word from Tobias all day, maybe the ship's security systems were all fixed, there was nothing to worry about. Sabella thought she would pop up on deck to check before darkness fell. Closing her door, she made her way down the pillared corridor. It was so nice to walk in a straight line again after all the rocking and rolling from the storm. Climbing the stairs, she opened the door and stepped out into the fresh evening air, which was turning much colder by the day the further north they ventured. The deck was a hive of activity with equipment and tools scattered everywhere. Seeing her on deck, Tobias came over, looking very stressed and tired.

"How are things going?" Sabella asked.

"Not very well I'm afraid. The ship sustained a fair bit of damage in the storm, unfortunately most to its security systems. Everything else is working fine but of course we need to get the shields and lights working before the dead of night. We are still over the ridge and won't make shallow water until morning. We still have a few hours yet, now is not the time for giving up. We will keep working until the last minute."

"What happens if we can't fix it?" Sabella asked with a sound of terror in her voice.

"I won't lie to you, if the security systems are not up and running. The Compton is entering the unknown; we have never been in this situation so we don't know what the outcome will be for the Compton. All we can do is try and make the ship as safe as possible. Now we are reinforcing the vulnerable parts of the ship to make them stronger, should the worst happen, and we get attacked," Tobias said.

"I want to help, so what can I do?" Sabella asked.

Turning, he pointed, "Kaylum needs some help with the door; you can give him a hand if you like."

"Alright, I can do that. How long have we got?" Sabella asked.

Taking a watch from his pocket Tobias glanced at it, "We have four hours till the dead of night but can only be on deck for another two as after that it becomes too risky, so we better get on with it."

Walking over to Kaylum, Sabella helped him with fixing a thick steel door which when finished and shut would give an extra layer of protection leading inside the ship. The wheelhouse was also being clad in steel with only little slits being left so that Paiter could see out. It now resembled a tank rather than the wheelhouse of the ship.

As the next two hours rolled by it became too unsafe to be on deck, they had all done their best to make the ship as safe as possible. Darkness crept its way into the sky and Tobias ordered everyone below deck, even though they still had two hours till the dead of night. Stepping into the safety of the ship and out of the cold night air Sabella waited for Tobias to finish talking to Paiter. He then closed the wheelhouse door, locking the little robot inside behind all the extra steel plaiting. Walking across the deck Kaylum and Keltal stepped through the door followed by Tobias who pulled the now very heavy door closed and bolted it shut.

"Will it hold?" Sabella asked sounding extremely worried.

"I hope so," replied Tobias. "We have done all we can for now, we just have to get through the next few hours."

Climbing down the stairs into the pillared corridor they found the Professor waiting for them. He handed the twins a torch each and explained that they were miniature versions of the sunlight beam, like the one that ran around the outside of the Compton. In the event of anything getting into the ship these torches could be used, but as they were so powerful, they only had a limited life span, so were to only be used in emergencies. The twins took their torches and took up their positions at either end of the corridor.

"Right, Professor, you can go to your room now. Please lock your door," ordered Tobias. "That includes you, Sabella," he added turning to face her.

"I need you to also go into your quarters, lock the door and please don't come out until I call you. I mean what I say for your own safety and that of the orbs, you must not leave your room."

"I understand, I will do as you ask but can you please let me know when it's all clear and that we have passed safely through the dead of night," replied Sabella.

Turning, she opened her door and walked into her room. Taking one last look at a very worried Tobias who smiled at her half-heartedly, she closed the door and walked through to her bedroom sitting down on the end of the bed feeling absolutely helpless as the next two hours were crucial to the protection of the orbs and their voyage to the ice.

As the minutes ticked by, she paced up and down the room clock watching. It was like torture slowly watching the time make its way to ten minutes to twelve. Walking to her door she placed her ear up against it listening for any unusual noises, but there was only silence. Returning quickly back to look at the clock she now saw it was a couple of minutes to midnight. She suddenly felt the Compton list to port. Running back to her door she once again placed her ear against it. This time there was a lot of noise. A big fight was taking place outside in the corridor. It was clear that Mortigan's army had gotten onto the ship. Stepping back from the door she placed her head in her hands and didn't know what to do. She could go and help or stay here in her room like Tobias had asked her too. Hearing the noise slowly dying down then suddenly stop, she went to the door and called out.

"Hello Tobias? Keltal? Kaylum? Is everything alright?" But no answer came back. A decision had to be made, she chose to go against Tobias and open the door, after all if Tobias and everyone had been killed there was no way she could complete the mission on her own, so she decided if they were going to lose this fight, they would go down together.

Slowly, she opened the door peering out into the darkness for all the lights were out. Closing her eyes, she switched her mind to night vision sight and instantly could see everything in the pillared corridor. There was no one there just lots of ash from destroyed viper warriors which rose up into the air as she walked down towards the steps. It was then that she came face to face with her first warrior that was jumping down the stairs snorting and growling at her. Walking towards her it held out its weapon and prepared to attack. Without thinking she stepped towards it. She wasn't afraid, scared or intimidated by this ugly creature. As it lunged at her with its sword it felt like everything was in slow motion, almost as if she could easily move out of the way. Time and time again the creature tried, swinging and stabbing at her but every time she just stepped aside. Finally frustrated the warrior jumped in the air, sword above its head, attempting one big strike. Stepping to the side she reached out and hit the warrior with the palm of her hand instantly making it crumble to the floor in a pile of ash.

Realising her new-found power, she opened her eyes and ran up the steps destroying more warriors on her way. Reaching the door, she jumped out onto a battlefield. There were hundreds of warriors attacking the ship and crew. Seeing their main target, a lot of them turned and came towards her but again it all felt very easy like slow motion and she could easily deal with their attacks, each one being vaporised.

Not being able to move as she was now surrounded, Sabella looked down the deck of the Compton. She could see the twins fighting hard and destroying dozens of warriors each but many more were coming over the side. It was then she saw Tobias stumble and fall from behind the wheelhouse. Led on his back he was doing his best to fight them off but it was only a matter of time. She could see he had been injured and when a warrior jumped on top of him raising its weapon above his head, she knew he was about to die.

Raising her hand, she shouted for the warrior to stop. A fire bolt shot from her palm blasting its way across the deck, destroying warriors as it went turning everything to ash including the one on top of Tobias. Amazed at herself she turned and released more bolts of fire, shooting each one down the deck of the Compton vaporizing hundreds of warriors. It was then that the dead of night finished. Every one of the remaining warriors that couldn't make it back over the side started crumbling, eventually turning to very neat piles of ash on the deck.

Running over to Tobias she bent down. He had his eyes shut and she feared the worst, "Tobias can you hear me? It's me Sabella."

"I know who it is, I thought I told you to stay in your room. Are you ever going to listen to me?" Tobias replied a broad grin spreading across his face. Slowly, sitting up he looked at his arm which was injured and bleeding.

"We need to get you down to the Professor so he can have a look at you," said Sabella.

"I'm okay," he winced. "It's Paiter who needs the help." He said pointing across the deck to where the little robot lay badly broken and damaged. Getting to his feet and being joined by Kaylum and Keltal they all walked across to the stricken robot. He had lost an arm and little blue sparks could be seen through holes in his outer shell where he had been attacked. He was trying to speak but all the words were coming out all mumbled and jumbled.

Turning, Tobias looked at the twins. "Well done, you two, you both did very well. Kaylum can you take control of the Compton and steer us on a safe passage until Paiter is well enough to resume control?"

"Will do, Captain," he replied.

"Keltal, can you carry Paiter down to the Professor for me?"

Bending down the giant picked up the little broken robot and they made their way down below deck to the laboratory. Looking around, Sabella spotted Paiter's arm, carefully making her way through the now dispersing piles of ash, bent down and picked it up before quickly following the others. Waiting for them at his door, the Professor ushered them into a table he had cleared in preparation for their arrival. Looking worried and upset he helped them lay Paiter down before connecting him up to machines and monitors. Jester had also arrived, he walked over and placed a hand on his brother's head. Sabella could feel the pain and sadness he was feeling so she made her way over to him and bent down, placing a comforting arm around him.

"I'm so sorry Jester I really don't know what to say. You must stay with your brother, don't worry about me. You can stay with him for as long as it takes, for he is the most important thing at the moment. So as from now you are relieved from all your duties."

"Will he be alright?" the little robot asked.

"I can't answer that I'm afraid, only the Professor can, once he has patched up Tobias, he will do all he can to make Paiter as good as new. If you need me for anything you know where I am." Standing up, she left her little robot servant to watch over his brother and turned to the Professor who had just finished mending Tobias' arm, with some magic spray, which when put on worked quickly in repairing the wound. It now looked nearly as good as new. Standing up Tobias stretched out his arm to test all was working properly.

"Thank you, Professor; you have done a good job there. I will leave you in peace now as I know you want to attend to Paiter. I will pop back first thing in the morning to see how he is getting on. Come on, Sabella; let's leave so the Professor can get started."

Stepping out through the door, Sabella looked back at a very sad Professor who was in for a very long night, trying to save one of his own creations.

Chapter 13

Sitting on the edge of her bed, Sabella rubbed her eyes and stretched. Apart from images of a black wave which were occurring nightly now it had been a reasonably good night's sleep, after the chaos of the night before. Looking towards the end of the bed she missed not seeing the big round eye of her servant robot Jester peering back at her. She just hoped it all went well with Paiter during the night and that the Professor had performed some magic on him. With a hot bath and some clean clothes on she walked through the big doors into the training room, making her way over to the turquoise pools. It was obvious to her now that these pools were part of her culture and not that of Knighton, they had a purpose but there was still so much more she had to discover.

Just then a shimmering image in the corner signalled the arrival of Marmaduke, slowly becoming clearer.

"Morning, Marmaduke," said Sabella.

"Good morning, Sabella," replied the little grey-haired old man, "I take it you are well after your adventurous last few days. I have heard a lot about you."

"You have been talking to Tobias," she joked.

"Well yes, but after all, you did go against his word. But on the other hand, you did save the ship and crew so we don't need to go over it, do we?! All I will say is very well done, you showed immense bravery in the face of danger, we are very proud of you. What I am interested in is your powers, I would never have imagined them to be so advanced so soon. So for this morning's training session, you can impress me with your new-found skills. I will put an image of a warrior in the room, you can practise hitting it."

"Okay, I can do that," Sabella answered.

"Let's begin," said her teacher.

Looking around the room for any sign of the creature Sabella suddenly caught a glimpse of one out of the corner of her eye appearing from behind a pillar. Holding her arm up with the palm of her hand pointing forward she fired a bolt of fire. Flying across the room it exploded against the wall. Just then another warrior appeared, so spinning quickly she shot a second bolt of fire, then a third. More and more appeared, she had to twist and turn rapidly to get them all. It was then that Marmaduke upped it all and turned out the lights. Quickly, shutting her eyes she could easily pick out the black lifeless shapes moving towards her as she fired off more fireballs. But Marmaduke was intent on testing her so he overwhelmed her with warriors. There were now at least a hundred, if not more circling her. Even putting her other hand up and firing from both she couldn't stop them moving ever closer. "There's too many," Sabella shouted, "I can't contain them all."

"Stop," shouted her teacher. Instantly the room came to a standstill and fell silent before the lights were turned back on.

Sabella opened her eyes, "There's too many of them I'm not fast enough to get them all. What happens if I'm in this situation for real?" she asked worryingly

"You will be," replied Marmaduke. "At some point in your life you may face a whole army of warriors so that's why I have put you in this situation."

"So what is the answer?" Sabella asked.

"Firstly, you need to stay calm nothing will happen if you cloud your mind with panic. Your thoughts should be as clear as the crystal pool. Now remember your training, place your arms down by your side, the palms of your hands facing the floor and slowly turn your upper body. Stay focused you have the power so use it. I will start the warriors once more, are you ready? Unleash your power."

Seeing the army moving ever closer she believed in Marmaduke and in her own ability. Slowly turning from side to side she thought of fire, a raging inferno was being lit inside her stomach and crept up her body, before flowing down her arms and exploding out of her hands in constant stream of flames. The flames circled her and crept outwards, almost as if a stone was thrown into a still pool of water and the ripples had moved outwards to the edge. The flames were fanning outwards engulfing anything in its path. Including every warrior which burst into flames the moment it was touched.

"Stop," shouted Marmaduke once more.

Turning to face her teacher, Sabella noticed he looked extremely happy with a big smile on his face.

"You have mastered the power of fire, Sabella. All we need to do now is practise your skills in the remaining days of the voyage. By the time you reach Stenbury, I hope it will be second nature to you. It's just a shame we will not have time to go through the remaining three orbs but time has been very much against us. I hope on your speedy and safe return that we can learn the remaining orbs at a more leisurely pace. So that concludes your training for today. I will see you again tomorrow when we will go through the finer points of your skill, unless you have any questions for me?"

"I do have one question, when I was fighting the viper warriors, everything seemed very slow as if it was all in slow motion," said Sabella.

"That's an easy one to answer," replied Marmaduke, "The fact is as a sorceress you are a lot faster than mere mortals. Have you ever tried to swat a fly and it always gets away?"

"Yes," Sabella answered.

"Well it's the same principle. The fly was a lot faster than you, and could easily dodge your intents to squash it, but don't think for one minute that all warriors will be that slow. You were just fortunate to come across an untrained or badly trained army. The closer you get to Mortigan, the tougher and better trained they will become. So as I say to you all the time, practice is everything. You are slow in terms of where you will be with training."

"I understand," Sabella replied. "Thank you, I will see you tomorrow."

The image of her teacher faded and disappeared. Closing the door to her training room she turned and walked over to her talk tube, picking it up she pulled out the cork and called Tobias.

"Morning, Sabella," a gruff voice said on the other end.

"Morning," Sabella replied, "I have just finished training, can I come up on deck for a little while?"

"Of course, you can," Tobias answered. "But I think you should go and see Paiter first. It's good news so don't worry. I think you might be surprised. Anyway, I think the Professor would like to see you."

"Alright then I shall go there first then come up on deck." Placing the talk tube back on the wall she walked over to her front door, opened it and stepped out. She made her way towards the laboratory and saw that the door was open, so she popped her head around the corner. "Morning, Professor."

"Morning, Sabella," he squeaked, beckoning her in. "Come in."

Walking over to the table she could see that Paiter was still laid out. "How is he, Professor?"

"Ask him yourself," he replied excitedly.

Leaning forward, she could see the little robot had been polished to a high shine. Gone were the holes and gashes from the night before, he was now looking as good as new. "Hello, Paiter, how are you feeling?"

Turning his head, he looked at her.

"I'm fine thanks to the Professor. I'm hoping to be back on the bridge and in control of the Compton by tonight. It's also nice to have my arm back, thank you for finding it for me."

"That's a pleasure, it's good to see you fighting fit and back with us." Turning, Sabella looked at the Professor. "You have done an amazing job on him, is he really alright to go back to work?"

"Apart from an oil and fluid change which he is having right now, he is a hundred percent fit. Jester has also had a service during the night and is now up on deck with Tobias and the twins helping to tidy up the damage," said the Professor.

"In that case, I better get up there so I can help as well," Sabella hurried along.

"Before you go, I need to give you something that you are going to need," said the Professor.

Walking over to his desk, he picked up a red coat and handed it to her.

"What's this?" Sabella asked.

"As we sail further north," the Professor explained. "It's going to get colder, a lot colder. This coat I have made for you should help keep you warm and I also have trousers, boots and gloves which you don't need just yet. Why don't you try it on?"

Taking the coat, Sabella slipped it on to find that it was very long, almost reaching down to her feet, but amazingly it was very light. The Professor explained that it was filled with a special material which would help keep the weight down, even if the coat got wet. Also between the outer and inner layers, a network of wires ran so that when a button was pressed on a battery pack which sat in the inner pocket, it would warm the coat up. But it was to only be used in emergencies as it only had a short life span.

"I like it, Professor, it fits fine. Does the colour suit me?" she asked jokingly doing a twirl. "I might as well keep it on while I go up on deck. Thank you, Professor, I will see you later," Sabella said, before leaving him to get on with his work on Paiter.

Walking down the corridor and up the stairs she stepped out onto the deck. There was a stiff breeze, also she noticed that the steel sails had been opened once more. The Compton was flying along, she could hear the bow cutting its way through the waves as it powered forward, the old ship was once again looking like itself; gone were the big metal plates that covered everything. The wheelhouse had been fixed up with new glass and the hole in the roof patched up. All the brass and copper had been polished to a high shine and the twins were now fixing the very last piece of broken railing. Tobias was back towards the stern. On seeing her approach, he stood up from what he was doing. "I like the coat," he laughed with a big smile on his face.

"Yours isn't bad either," she laughed back. "But at least mine is a better colour," Sabella said referring to her red one, rather than a dowdy brown colour.

"Yes," Tobias agreed. "I don't think I would look good in red. You have to agree they are very warm."

"How cold is it going to get?" Sabella asked.

"Very cold," Tobias grumbled. "At least minus twenty if not lower. But the Professor has informed me that our coats can cope with temperatures as low as minus sixty so we should be alright."

"How's the Compton now?" Sabella enquired, referring to all the damage.

"She's fine, everything is working perfectly and being as we will be back in shallow water again in the next hour or two, I can't see us having any more problems in the remainder of our voyage," hoped Tobias.

"How long do you think we have got?" said Sabella.

"At our current speed no more than a few days, but that is only to the outer edge of the ice field. It might take a couple more days to slowly pick our way through the pack ice and once we can't go any further, we shall then have to go on foot."

"Sorry to ask so many questions but how long will that take?"

"That's the hard one, if it was as the crow flies, then not long, but we have no idea what lies in our way; mountains of ice, crevices, blizzards and icy winds so cold that they freeze you solid within a second. We may encounter them all, we only have a very old map to go on. Since it was drawn a lot may have changed. It's going to be very hard going but if we can get there as quick as possible, plant the bomb and get back safe then I will be happy."

"That makes two of us," Sabella smiled, "Is it alright if I stay up on deck for a while?"

"Of course, it is," Tobias replied. "It's getting a lot safer now with the nights becoming very short. In a couple more days it will be continuous daylight but to be on the safe side stay where I can see you."

Walking to the stern of the Compton, Sabella sat down on a large winch and looked out across the wide-open expanse of sea. It had been such a long time since she had seen land, in a strange way she was quite looking forward to stepping onto firm ground, even if it was a freezing cold island of ice.

Chapter 14

A deep rumbling sound woke Sabella from her sleep, sitting up she listened intently. Time and time again a noise echoed through the ship. The last few days had gone well without any problems, so what could be making this sound. Climbing out of bed she got dressed, put her coat on and stepped out into the pillared corridor. Still she could hear the noise but couldn't work out where it was coming from. Stopping at Tobias' door, she knocked twice but there was no answer. Perhaps he was up on deck investigating the strange noise himself she thought. Walking to the stairs she climbed them and stepped out through the door at the top into very bright sunlight. There was not a breath of wind but it was still bitterly cold. Tobias had joked that sometimes it was so cold the words would freeze when they came out of your mouth. Looking around she noticed big long icicles hanging off the wheelhouse. Each one about a foot long, shining like a jewel in the sunlight

"Sabella," called Tobias. "Over here."

Walking over to him she took hold of the rail and peered over the side. The sea was a lovely deep sky-blue colour, completely flat, not even a ripple could be seen. She also found what was causing the noise in the ship. The bow of the Compton was hitting large lumps of ice which were floating in the sea in front of them. Some were much bigger than others and Tobias was guiding Paiter who was back in control of the helm around the larger ones.

"I take it the ice woke you?" Tobias asked.

"Why do you ask that?" Sabella smiled.

"Because, Sabella, it's only three thirty in the morning," Tobias laughed.

"Yes, I was woken by the noise; it's normally so quiet down below. Any noise now seems strange, but not as strange as seeing the sun in the sky at this time of night."

"Yes, it is a little weird, but we will not see night again for a while," said Tobias.

"Is this the ice field?" Sabella asked.

"No," Tobias replied. "This is just the outer edge. The pieces that you are seeing now are known as growlers. They are lumps that have broken off the main ice field and are floating out to sea where they slowly melt away. We won't hit the ice field for another three or four hours so I suggest you go back to bed and get some more sleep."

"I think I will, but what about you Tobias, you look shattered," Sabella said, feeling like she should stay.

"I'm alright, once we hit the main ice field one of the twins will take over and I will get some rest," Tobias answered, looking exhausted.

With a numb face and cold hands Sabella headed below deck to the warmth of her large bed and fell back to sleep.

A few more hours had passed, Sabella woke once more to the familiar smell of bacon sandwiches. Sitting up she reached over and took one off the plate. She couldn't see Jester but she could hear him moving about in the library cleaning and tidying. Swinging her legs off her bed, still dressed in her coat, she walked through to see him.

"Morning, Jester," said Sabella.

"Morning, Sabella," replied the little robot from behind a big pile of books.

"What are you doing?" she asked.

"I had some spare time so I thought I would clean and tidy all the books. I have to look after them as they are very old, also extremely fragile," Jester answered.

"You're doing a fantastic job there, Jester, and thank you for my bacon sandwich. I'm going to go back up on deck now to see Tobias."

"You can't, Sabella, I was just about to call you. Marmaduke needs to see you as soon as possible." Jester showing urgency.

"Did he say if it was anything important?" Sabella asked sounding alarmed.

"No, he just asked me to wake you and send you in to meet him," Jester said, realising he had worried Sabella.

"Thanks, Jester, I better go straight in then." Sabella walked over to the doors of her training room, pushed them open and walked in. Closing them behind her she walked over to the crystal pool and sat down on the edge. She lowered her hand into the water which felt very strange compared to normal water; this was more like runny glue. As she swished her hand about it left a white trail behind before turning back to a deep blue colour. Even when she lifted her hand out of the water it took a little while for it to run off her fingers, but when it did it left her hand bone dry. It obviously had a role to play in this whole mess of a jigsaw she had been thrown into but until she could work it out it would have to stay a mystery. Looking up she noticed the shimmering figure of Marmaduke appearing at the end of the room.

"Morning, Sabella," said the old man. "Thank you for coming so quick."

"I take it, it must be important for you to call me at this time of morning?" Sabella queried.

"It is important to me, I needed to see you for anytime now you will enter the ice field. There the Compton will be too far north for my image to reach you so until you sail back into open water, I will no longer be able to communicate. I'm hoping the small amount of time we have had together, has helped you realise who you are and what you are capable of. Also I hope I have helped guide you on the path to fulfilling your destiny. I'm sorry that time has been against us, but be assured, young Sabella, I have great confidence in your ability as a sorceress, the orbs are in good hands with you as their protector."

"Thank you, Marmaduke, your words mean a lot to me. It does feel a lot like I have been thrown in at the deep end but with your help, guidance and the support of the fantastic crew I have here aboard the Compton, we will do whatever it takes to complete the mission, I will not let you down, and return home safely to Castle Cove." Sabella's voice carried a heavy load.

Just then the image of her teacher faded and crackled. In a broken distorted voice Marmaduke offered her some last words of advice before disappearing completely. Looking around, she thought how strange it was going to be from now on not having her daily routine of training, at least not until they made it back from the ice anyway.

Closing the door to her training room she walked past Jester who was still head deep in books, out of her quarters along the corridor and up the stairs before stepping out into the freezing air once more. Walking forward to where Tobias was, she could see a lot had changed in the time since she was last up here. Gone were the growlers which slowly drifted along on currents and now replacing them was a sea of ice. For as far as the eye could see it was just a carpet of white. Slowly coming to a stop, the Compton was now sitting on the very edge of the ice field.

"Is this where we get off?" Sabella asked.

"No," replied Tobias. "It's far too dangerous the ice is still too thin. You can't see it but it's still moving all the time. Big cracks quickly open up then close again. If anyone of us fell in, it's certain death. We are much better on the Compton until we can go no further. Only then will we go by foot."

"Won't the ice damage the ship?" Sabella asked.

"Normally yes but the Professor has fitted a new shield come ice breaker to the front of the Compton. I haven't seen it myself yet so let's deploy it," Tobias answered waving his arm above his head as a signal to Paiter who in turn pulled a leaver. As the pair of them leaned over the front, a hatch opened up at the top of the bow. Slowly, a banana shaped steel girder with spikes on it came out and curved around the bow before going under the water line, locking into place.

"Well I'm most impressed with that," smiled Tobias. "I just hope it works as good as it looks." Turning, he looked towards the wheelhouse. "All ahead, slow please, Paiter."

"Will do, Captain," shouted back the little robot.

The big paddles on either side slowly started to turn edging the ship ever closer to the ice. There was a slight bump, gradually the ship rose up. The silence and stillness were then broken by the deep cracking sound of the ice being ripped apart by the bow of the Compton. Moving forward through the sea of white the path they had cut out began closing instantly behind them leaving no trace of where they had been.

"Right that's me done," yawned Tobias. "I'm now off to bed. Kaylum can take over."

"I'm going back to my quarters as well. I can't feel my fingers and my face is numb," replied Sabella.

Leaving Kaylum to his post she headed back down below to the warmth of her quarters. Taking off her coat she rubbed her hands together which tingled as they started to warm up. Walking into the library she sat down with a book and sipped on a steaming mug of hot chocolate which Jester had so kindly conjured up. She would spend many more hours at her desk reading in the next couple of days. Firstly it meant she could stay in, out of the ever-worsening weather, and secondly she could catch up on her studies. But with the ice field getting thicker and the Compton getting slower it was only a matter of time before they came to a grinding halt.

Chapter 15

Walking across the library, Sabella picked up her talk tube.

"Hello?"

"Hello, Sabella, it's Tobias. I'm heading up on deck as the Compton has come to a stop and we can go no further. We will have to assess the situation but I think we are going to have to leave the ship to continue on foot."

"Alright, I will just put my coat on and head up to meet you. See you in a minute," said Sabella.

Hanging the talk tube back on the wall Sabella put on her coat, gloves, hat and specially made boots as she headed up on deck. Stepping out the door she was greeted by an eerie scene. The Compton had become part of the ice field, everything from the wheelhouse to the deck and the masts had been covered in a white icy sheet. Nothing had escaped for even Paiter had a covering of ice on him. The ship was surrounded by a low-lying fog which eerily moved across the ice like a giant monster engulfing everything in its path. Big snowflakes gradually made their way down from the seemingly cloudless, dull grey sky. The ice field around them cracked and groaned under the immense pressures.

Walking over to Tobias and the twins, Sabella peered over the side of the ship. The Compton was indeed stuck fast, no sea could be seen around it. The ice field had moved in and clamped the ship in a vice-like grip.

"It's not going to crush the ship is it?" Sabella asked.

"I hope not," replied Tobias.

"The Compton is a strong ship although I didn't think the ice field would have been this thick so soon. Anyway we can't dwell on that now, we must make plans to leave the ship and carry on by foot. The Professor has assured me that he will do all he can to free the Compton for when we get back. Our job is to plant the bomb, so we must all go gather our bits and meet back on deck in five minutes." Tobias sounding critical of time.

Doing as Tobias asked, Sabella headed back to her quarters where she found Jester waiting for her, with a fully stacked rucksack. Everything she needed for the journey had been neatly packed inside including a couple of surprise treats. Gathering all her things she bent down in front of her little robot.

"Thanks for all you have done Jester, I will see you soon," said Sabella with a slightly frightened tone to her voice.

"Please come back safe, Miss Sabella," Jester replied, a little sadness in his voice.

"I will. I promise." Standing up she lifted her rucksack onto her shoulder, had a final look around her room and headed back up onto deck. Once there she saw that Tobias had opened a hatch in the deck where a small crane had appeared from. Pressing a button, the crane whirled away and lifted a sledge like vehicle out from the ship's hull. Swinging it over the side it was lowered down onto the ice and was shortly followed by a second sledge before Tobias stowed the crane away and closed the hatch once more.

Kaylum lowered a rope ladder over the side and climbed down onto the ice. Keltal then passed all of their equipment down to him where he packed it onto the sledges including the freeze bomb which had been packed in its own special box. Then Keltal and Tobias descended also, lastly followed by Sabella who stepped off the last rung onto the ice. It felt very strange being off the ship for the first time in what seemed like ages, but not as strange as the feeling of the ice moving under her feet. Very slowly it would rise up then sink back down. It would creak and groan as all the forces worked against each other. Small cracks would appear as the ice split then instantly close back up.

"It's time for us all to leave," ordered Tobias. "Sabella, you're with me."

Walking over to the sledge she climbed aboard. The sledges weren't pulled by dogs instead they had a small engine out front where the dogs would normally be. It was attached by two long metal poles also steered and controlled by long reins. Tobias pulled a cord on the engine and it fired into life breaking the silence of the desolate land. As he wandered back to his seat in front of her he sat down and turned to Sabella.

"Remember what I told you, keep your face covered at all times, don't leave any skin showing or it will freeze," said Tobias very matter-of-factly.

Pulling her goggles down and the mask up Sabella felt her face in case any bit of skin was showing before Tobias was happy to go on.

"That's good," Tobias shouted, "Now hold tight, don't let go."

Turning back in his seat he took hold of the reins, glanced over at the twins to make sure they were ready, and headed off. Slowly at first but gradually the engine's revs picked up, so did their speed. Side by side the two sledges sped across the ice field into a blanket of white snow. It was hard to see just where the sky and land joined.

Looking over her shoulder, Sabella got a last glimpse of the Compton through the snowy haze; the light in the wheelhouse shining like a beacon and the black hull of the ship gradually fading like a ghost into the white background. Finally disappearing from view completely she turned back around and tried to tuck herself in behind Tobias but it was never going to work, it was just too cold. Over the next part of their arduous journey they covered bumps, ridges and the occasional hole, which would have thrown her into the air if she hadn't been holding on tight. Also ice particles had started to form all over her, it felt like she was being frozen alive. Their journey had only just begun but already she was questioning her ability to see it through. So when Tobias came off the throttle and the sledges came to a steady stop, she breathed a sigh of relief. Climbing off the sledge Tobias turned and lifted up his goggles which had completely frozen over.

"Are you alright, Sabella?" Tobias asked.

"I'm okay; it's a bit uncomfortable but it looks as if you're suffering a lot worse up front than me," she said pointing to his goggles which had icicles hanging from them.

"That's the reason I had to stop," Tobias smiled.

"I couldn't see where I was going. I definitely couldn't see the navigation device on my wrist," said Tobias.

"Oh I did wonder how you knew which way to go when everything is white and there is nothing to fix your bearings on," said Sabella with a frown upon her face.

"Yes, this little gadget here is something the Professor made me," Tobias said lifting his arm up.

"It's like a wrist watch with a circle of arrows on it, the one that's red," Tobias explained.

"It will always point to the spot where we have to plant the bomb. When all of them are red we have arrived at the spot and if I press this button it will guide us back to the position of the ship."

"Does it tell you how far away we are?" Sabella asked.

"Unfortunately not but I do know one thing," said Tobias trying to sound encouraging.

"What's that?" Sabella queried.

"My instincts are telling me we are heading into an ice storm," Tobias didn't want to alarm Sabella more than he needed to at this point.

"How do you know that?" said Sabella.

"I don't really it's just the way the wind is picking up and the visibility is getting a lot less. If we can make it to this point," Tobias said, pointing to an area on the very old map.

"We can set up camp, have some food and take much needed rest, so we better go."

Climbing back on board their sledges and heading off once more they had to endure more treacherous conditions before the weather started closing in around them. Although it was cold, the special coats the Professor had made for them were holding the worst of it at bay, but as the storm closed in around them, the visibility became zero, the temperature started to drop, and fast. The sledges were slowing down to a crawl. They tried desperately to carry on but the storm was so severe that the little engines could no longer sustain enough heat to keep themselves going and in an instant, they froze solid bringing them to a stop.

Climbing off, Tobias turned to Sabella. "Press the button in your coat or you will freeze to death, we need to get the tents up," he shouted

Turning around, she grabbed her rucksack and stepped off the sledge. Instantly she was blown off her feet by the ferocious wind, rolling over a couple of times she finished face down in the snow. Struggling to her feet and bracing herself against the force of the wind she pushed the button in her pocket. Instantly, the coat started to warm up and force the cold back out, but the warm pleasure was soon replaced by blind terror for so bad was the visibility she had lost sight of the others, and in her panic she forgot all about her special vision. They were only a few feet away but she daren't move, a couple of steps in the wrong direction and she could be lost forever. Turning around, she shouted their names, but against this howling wind her voice barely left her mouth. Just then a very large hand from one of the twins grabbed her shoulder and pulled her backwards into the safety of a tent. Instantly, there was relief from the torturous conditions from outside. Pulling off her goggles and hat she looked at the other three.

"Thank you whoever that was," Sabella said.

"It was Kaylum," replied Tobias.

"Well thank you Kaylum, I can't believe just how quick it closed in around us and how bitterly cold it has got." Sabella sounding so very grateful.

"I think it surprised us all," said Tobias.

"What we need to do now is eat and drink something. Most of all we must all get some rest while we can. It's impossible to go on until the storm breaks."

Opening her rucksack Sabella looked in and remembered Jester had said something about some surprises being in there. Finding a little packet all wrapped up and tied with string she opened it and immediately started to laugh.

"What's so funny?" asked Tobias.

"It's just Jester, he's so sweet; he tries his best to make sure everything is perfect. He was so happy that he had put some surprise packets in my rucksack but I dread to think what's in the other ones," said Sabella.

"Why what's in that one?" Tobias asked.

Reaching forward Sabella laid the packet of cold fish and chips in front of them.

"Oh, I see what you mean," smiled Tobias.

But the twins just couldn't see the funny side of things as they had never seen fish and chips before. They didn't understand that they needed to be hot. Leaning forward Tobias grabbed a big fat chip and stuffed it into his mouth.

"Oh, how I miss chips even if they are cold."

Still not seeing the funny side, Kaylum leant forward.

"Captain, what's a chip? Is it something from your world?"

"It is," Tobias mumbled stuffing another one into his mouth.

"Please try one the pair of you," Sabella said pushing the packet towards them. "You can also tell me what you think of the fish." She added trying not to burst out laughing as she pointed to the brown wrinkly battered thing.

Looking at each other horrified the twins turned and said at the same time. "That's a fish?"

Reaching forward Keltal prodded it.

"That's the strangest looking creature I have ever seen. It's got no eyes, mouth or fins. I'm not eating that."

"Nor am I," replied his brother.

"Try a chip then," said Sabella who was now giggling uncontrollably.

Tobias was also doing his best not to laugh but his big rosy cheeks and watery eyes were a clue he was about to burst. So when the twins finally plucked up the courage to try a chip each Sabella and Tobias looked on knowing what was about to happen, and it did. Popping the chips into their mouths the two giants started to chew. Keltal was the first to screw his face up slowly followed by Kaylum who was so disgusted by the taste that he spat it across the tent.

"That was the most horrible thing I have ever tasted," Kaylum bellowed.

"Well I think they are splendid," said Tobias picking another up and popping it into his mouth. "What do you think, Sabella?"

"I think this fish is lovely," Sabella replied as she bit off a large piece of fish. The two of them fell about laughing. Eventually they did calm down and with the warmth returning to her hands and feet. Sabella wrapped herself up in her blanket, and with the wind howling around the tent she drifted off to sleep.

Chapter 16

Opening her eyes, Sabella looked up at the inside of the tent. The bright sun which was shining against the material was only through one side. The other was covered with a thick layer of snow which had built up during the storm. It now made the tent sag down to about an inch off the face of Tobias, who was snoring deeply, along with the twins.

The wind and snow had long since ceased. For once it looked and sounded calm outside. Suddenly she noticed a shadow go past the tent. Sitting up she looked at the material, scanning the outside for any sign of movement. Maybe it was nothing, just a trick of the mind, or a cloud passing over the sun. It was clear there wasn't a living thing that could have survived out there in the storm. Suddenly, it happened again. She could clearly see the shadow of a figure slowly moving towards the tent. It definitely wasn't Tobias or the twins as they were in the tent with her, so who or what was this figure looming largely over them? Whispering to Tobias, followed by the twins she got no response. It was then that she heard a low grumbling sound like growling.

It was clear this was not human and could only mean danger, so leaning back she lifted her arm taking aim at the ghostly figure which was now directly over them. Concentrating hard she built up the fire inside of her before firing a flaming bolt out the palm of her hand. In a flash the tent disappeared. Jumping up she fired another at the large hairy creature that was now running away in fear of its life. As it ducked down behind a large chunk of ice, she fired one more for good measure. Sabella exploded the ice with such force that water and steam shot high into the air.

"Sabella, what was it?" shouted Kaylum picking up his sword and looking around still a little dazed.

"It's over there behind that large chunk of ice. It's a huge creature. It's growling like a dog," said Sabella.

Kaylum turned to his brother, "Keltal lets go, there is no time we have to destroy it. We don't know what it is capable of. You circle that way and I will go this way. Sabella, you stay here."

"I wouldn't bother; it's harmless," came a voice from beneath a pile of snow. In the destruction of the tent, the snow which had built up on one side had caved in and covered Tobias. Sitting up he looked around.

Walking over, Sabella took his hand and helped him to his feet. Shaking himself off, he wiped his eyes and looked at her.

"Maybe I should have told you about them. They are known as the abominable snowmen. They are very harmless, shy creatures that roam the ice fields. I don't think that one will be bothering us again after your display of fire power."

"I didn't realise, I really thought it was something that could hurt us. I'm so sorry about the state of the tent. I'm over cautious for what's out there."

"You have been trained well. Please do not worry; we have spare ones. Now let's pack up our things, it is time to move on quickly we have been here too long," replied Tobias.

Picking up her rucksack Sabella swung it up onto her back and tied it at the front. Tobias dug his out from beneath the snow, and the twins who had now calmed down from their exchange with the abominable snowman, grabbed a handle each of the freeze bomb, and carefully lifted it.

Heading off the sun shone down on them from the cloudless blue sky, they walked across the crisp ice, leaving the sledges behind, frozen in time, and slowly being devoured by the ice. It was only a matter of time before they would disappear completely.

Looking forward, Sabella noticed the flat open baron ice field would soon be replaced by a more challenging landscape, and beyond that a mountain awaited them. Although it would take some time to get there, it seemed so much closer as the land met the sky. Coming to an abrupt halt at the edge of a glacier Tobias turned around to face them.

"We will stop here briefly and have something to eat and drink, then carry on as we must make the most of the good weather. It could turn nasty at any time so we need to keep moving," said Tobias.

Sitting next to a small trapped iceberg Sabella couldn't help but notice the piercing shades of sapphire due to the sunlight passing through the dense compacted ice. Opening her rucksack, she took out some biscuits but they tasted like cardboard. Tobias had assured her that they were high in carbohydrates and vitamins, they didn't taste too bad once they were dunked into a hot drink which itself had a strange taste. What Sabella wouldn't do for the taste of a cup of tea!

Standing up, Tobias walked over to where she was sat, holding out his hand he helped her to her feet.

"We need to get going, how are you feeling?"

"I'm fine, better now I can feel the sun on my face, although it is still bitterly cold. At least the wind has stopped which at times has been unbearable," said Sabella.

"I know what you mean," Tobias replied, "I hope that the next part of the journey should be a little easier on you."

"Which direction are we heading now?" Sabella asked.

"We will head towards the glacier," Tobias said pointing in front of him, "Towards the foot of the mountain you can see in the distance. There we will get some rest before the final push to the spot where we need to plant the bomb," Tobias said as he helped her on with her rucksack.

They gathered their things and headed off once more. The dead, flat ice field had now been replaced with a slight climb which wasn't much at first but became steeper as they headed up the ever-changing landscape. Eventually, it flattened out and they walked down towards a very impressive wall of ice called a wind scoop. It's where at its most extreme the wind carves out clefts between the glaciers. It reminded Sabella of a huge wave coming towards them, it looked as though it was about to break before being frozen in time.

Eventually, they walked out from beneath the wind scoop where it opened into a deep wide valley which stretched out in front of them all the way to the mountain which now stood high above them. So high that it had a ring of cloud covering the top.

Sabella just hoped they wouldn't have to climb it, and that there would be another way around or through the mountain of rock and snow. She had a strange feeling that things were going to get a whole lot harder once they got there but for now, they would make the most of the calm conditions and bright sunshine.

It was well below freezing, once again ice had formed on her face, mask and goggles. Under foot the hard ice crunching with every step they took. They were on a slight decline into the bottom of the valley which meant they were making very good progress that was until they reached the lowest point.

It was there that all the fine, powdery snow lay in wait for them. Slowly, the hard, icy crust gave way to a deep energy sapping sea of white slush; it was as if they were walking through quick sand. First it came up to their ankles, but as it crept up their legs and passed their knees, walking forward became impossible.

"We need to get our snow shoes on quickly," ordered Tobias.

Sitting down on the snow Sabella reached back and slid her snowshoes from her rucksack. One by one she fixed the tennis racket shaped shoes to her feet and tied them tightly. The next problem was getting back up. Try as she might it took a hand from Tobias to get her back onto her feet whilst she was still sliding around unable to regain her balance.

Setting off once more, it soon become clear to them that the final push to the foot of the mountain was going to be an arduous marathon. Every step she took had to be over emphasised to compensate for big round snowshoes. Slowly, her legs started to suffer, aching at first but as the lactic acid built up, the muscles in her legs started to stiffen the aching turned to a pain. They pushed on. The pain turned to a dull numbness, her legs didn't feel like her own, they felt as heavy as lead. Her walking had slowed to a wobbly shuffle. Fixing her eyes on the ground she blacked out everything around her including the pain and struggled on in a trance like state. It seemed to work eventually they entered the shadow of the mountain. Hidden from the sun the four of them carried on until they hit a wall of black rock stretching up as far as the eye could see to an eerie looking ring of grey clouds, which was slowly turning around the mountain top.

"We will stop here now for some food and rest," suggested Tobias.

The twins immediately started to erect a tent and although Sabella would have loved to have helped, she had stopped walking as her legs had seized solid. It was hard enough just bending down to take her shoes off but once she had she crawled into the tent and felt a huge sense of relief at finally having some rest. Lifting up her goggles, Sabella pulled them off and looked at the others who were already rummaging in their rucksacks, pulling out packets of food. Slipping her rucksack off her back she put her hand in and pulled out one of Jesters surprise food parcels. With the other three watching intently she opened it up, there in front of them sat a large piece of roast chicken.

"I don't even want to know what that is," moaned Keltal. "It looks disgusting, and as for trying it, you can forget it," added Kaylum.

"That's not fair," winged Tobias as he chewed on a large piece of salted dry fish that looked more like an old leather boot than something that had come out of the sea. "Are you sure you wouldn't want to swap, for this lovely piece of fish?" He smiled through gritted teeth.

Picking up the chicken leg Sabella took a large bite. "I think I will stick to this thank you," she smiled. "I would hate to take away your fish as you really look like your enjoying it."

"I thought you might say that, you have made the right choice this is disgusting. I wouldn't make my worst enemy eat this," Tobias grumbled.

Once they had stuffed themselves full of food and drink, they all settled down for their rest before the final push to where the bomb was to be planted. Climbing under her warm blanket it was hard to believe they had been travelling less than a day. It seemed and felt so much longer especially the way her body and legs were aching. Laying her head down she thought about Jester, Paiter and the Professor hoping they had managed to free the Compton from its icy grip, or had it all gone disastrously wrong and been crushed into a thousand pieces, disappearing under the ice forever. Whatever its fate, they had a job to do and when they woke from their short rest, the most dangerous part would begin.

Chapter 17

"Sabella, we need to go now," whispered Tobias waking her from her deep sleep.

"How long have we been here?" she grumbled from beneath her warm blanket.

"Not very long," replied Tobias, "But we need to carry on, the weather is still good and we have a tricky mountain path still to negotiate our way safely."

"I don't think my legs can carry me any further, they are really stiff and achy."

"They will loosen up once we start moving," Tobias smiled, "so come on and get yourself up; we have to go."

Sliding out from beneath her blanket she put on her hat, goggles crawled out from the tent into the eternal daylight. Sabella stood up on her very stiff legs. They were still in the shadow of the mountain. The sky was clear apart from the dark cloud that still hauntingly circled its top.

"Sabella, over here," called Tobias.

She slowly made her way over to the twins. They noticed they were standing next to a very small path. It was no wider than a metre and zigzagged up the sheer face of the black rock. A small arrow had been carved into the rock face to point them in the right direction although by the looks of it there was only one way and that was up.

"Right, Sabella," Tobias explained. "I will go first, you will follow me, Keltal then Kaylum can follow behind with the bomb. Please be careful, take special care with your footing as it might get very precarious. It's been many years since the last people trekked up the mountain side."

Stepping onto the path Tobias led them up the side of the mountain, as the path steepened he was right to have warned them. It was both dangerous and treacherous. Fragments of rock had fallen down over the years, covering the path which felt to them like they were walking on marbles. It didn't help that a lot of the path was frozen solid, but the scariest sections were where the path had fallen away. Thankfully someone had placed thick metal chains across the most dangerous stretches, so they had something to hold onto.

Very slowly they edged across the narrow parts, at times some were so thin that they had to put one foot in front of the other. The drop to their side was becoming ever steeper as the tents and equipment that they had left behind were now just a dot of colour in a sea of whiteness that stretched as far as the eye could see.

Tracing their route back Sabella could see the valley they had walked through and the ice sculpture far in the distance. Beyond that it became hazy but she could just pick out the edge of the ice field where the sledges had died. Coming to a sharp turn, Sabella noticed another arrow that had been carved into the wall.

"Tobias," she asked. "Who carved the arrows into the walls and put the chains up across the dangerous paths we had to cross? Surely people don't live here, do they?"

"No," Tobias replied. "No one could ever live here for any length of time. The arrows and chains have been here for many hundreds of years, they were placed here by your ancestors to help future generations find their way to the exact spot where Mortigan is entombed. You see there have been many scares over the centuries where the orbs have told us that the dark one is a threat. Your ancestors have had to come here to check he is still incarcerated and that all is safe. The good thing is, he has never managed to release himself from his tomb and we must make sure it is never going to happen in your time as sorceress."

"Isn't there a way we can put an end to all this?" Sabella questioned.

"Well if you mean can you kill him, many have tried but all have failed. Legend has it that many have fought the evil one face to face and none have lived to tell the story. He is just too powerful. Some have even said that he can't be killed, as he is immortal. So you can see why it is important to keep him entombed forever. At least that way we never have to know if he truly is immortal or not," said Tobias.

Deep down Sabella knew it was the right thing to do by planting the bomb, securing the safety and future of the orbs. That was how important this mission was. They had to keep the elements working as one, and most importantly to sustain life. Letting the darkness reign would destroy everything and condemn every living thing on every planet to a future of darkness and destruction.

As they trekked further up the mountain path it became slightly wider, making it easier to cope with the sheer drop which was now so high that just looking over the side made Sabella's stomach turn. After many more turns, scary moments with falling rocks, they turned the last corner. She noticed in front of them a long stone staircase that had been carved into the black rock. Stretching high up in front of them it disappeared into the grey cloud which still whirled around the mountaintop like some giant monster just above their heads. As they slowly made their way up the wide slippery steps, she noticed something else, it was getting warmer. The ice was melting and now instead of the rock being covered in snow it had green slime growing on it. It was as though they were stepping into another world. It was the smell that was the worst, it was foul. Lifting her hand up to her face she tried to cover her nose to mask it which was a blend of smelly feet and rotten eggs.

"What's that disgusting smell?" Sabella asked.

"I think it's this," answered Tobias poking a patch of the slimy green stuff which was growing on a rock next to him.

Instantly, his gloves started to smoke and melt. Quickly, he pulled his glove off and dropped it to the ground where within seconds it had fizzed and bubbled away to nothing.

"That is one dangerous substance," Tobias told them. "I think we better stay clear of that and all be careful with every step we take."

Continuing up the steep steps they started to enter the outer edges of the cloud. At first it was only wispy and swirled around them in patches but gradually they lost sight of the snowy valley that lay beneath them, the warm cloud thickened closing in around them and the sun slowly disappeared. There was no wind and it was deathly quiet. It felt like they were in a twilight zone which was a lot different from the bitterly cold, snowy wasteland they had just trekked across. It was grey, wet and miserable and still getting worse, to the point where they couldn't see the edge of the path. It was getting so bad now that their eyes were becoming useless.

"Stop!" ordered Tobias. "We need to close up and hold onto each other. I will carry on leading the way. We must stick together or one of us might get lost."

"How far is it?" Sabella asked.

"Not far I don't think; we just need to get to the cave entrance," said Tobias.

Sabella took hold of Tobias' coat and Kaylum took hold of hers with Keltal bringing up the rear. Slowly, they edged forward once more. It was a scary feeling knowing that a step in the wrong direction could send them all over the edge and to their death. Looking down they did their best to follow the path but it was painfully slow and inevitably they got lost.

"I think I've gone the wrong way," whispered Tobias, "I can't see the edges of the path anymore."

Bending down he tried his hardest to get them back on track but it was to no avail.

"What do we do now?" Sabella asked.

"We can't do anything but wait here and hope it clears a little so we can find our way again."

"I could use my vision powers to help us through," said Sabella.

"What's that?" shouted Kaylum interrupting her. "What's that? Who's there?"

"What's wrong?" called Tobias, as he turned around and strained his eyes into the mist.

"I saw something," shouted Kaylum. "A ghostly figure came up to me."

"Are you sure? I can hardly see my hand in front of my face. Maybe it was a trick of light or your mind."

"I have just seen it too," yelled Keltal as he let go of Sabella and drew his weapon.

"Let's just all calm down for a minute it's just the mist playing tricks on our mind," said Tobias but it was too late. The twins were scared, they feared for their safety and they started to panic, becoming defensive. Even with Tobias shouting at them to stop. Something was attacking them and they were fighting back.

Although Sabella couldn't see them fighting or what was attacking them, she was stood right next to them. One of her many untapped senses told her to lean back which she did and not a second too soon. Out of the mist in front of her eyes came the sharp edge of a blade, owned by one of the twins, who was flailing it about trying to hit the ghostly figure that moved within the mist. Dropping to the ground she crawled out of harm's way and had lost contact with Tobias who himself was now shouting and fighting. Kneeling up Sabella closed her eyes and used her night vision trying to catch a glimpse of any movement from within the dense cloud. Feeling pressure on her shoulders, she was pushed backwards onto the ground and pinned down. Opening her eyes, a haunting face now looked down on her, moving slowly down towards her until it was only an inch away. It had no features as such, it was like the mist had come to life and taken the shape of a human. It had immense strength. No matter how much she fought and struggled she couldn't fight it off.

"What do you want with us?" Sabella shouted.

"We need your living bodies," it replied in a haunting voice.

"Why our bodies?" Sabella asked under its tight grip.

"We died here on this mountain many hundreds of years ago, and now we are here in the mist waiting until the living come along. It will now be your turn to walk here alone until the next living passes by."

The figure then moved forward like it was trying to take over her body. Her bones felt like they were turning to ice as a pain shot through her. She was being taken over by another soul and she didn't know how to fight it. All of a sudden everything went quiet and Sabella began to wonder if it was all over. Had she been banished from her body and was now destined to spend the next hundred or so years as another lost soul wandering in the mountain mist.

Opening her eyes, she was slightly relieved to see that the ghostly being had not managed to snatch her soul but was now standing over her.

"Who are you?" It roared with a ferocious sound. "Where are you from?"

Slowly getting to her feet she looked at the haunting image before her knowing that she was far too powerful for it, and that she easily repelled any attempt from these body snatchers. However, she wasn't too sure about the others and knew she had to save them.

"My name is Sabella, I am head sorceress and guardian of the orbs. You will step back and let us have safe passage to the cave without fear of attack." He leaned towards her menacingly.

Holding her arms out straight with her palms upwards Sabella generated a burning fireball in her hands.

"If you do not let us pass, then I shall destroy everything and banish the mist in which you walk."

Hearing her warning and stepping back the ghost slowly started to part the mist around them. They were now stood in a pocket of clear air. By looking up through the funnel of cloud Sabella could see clear blue sky. As the misty cloud crept back further it revealed the twins who were standing back to back fighting off the retreating figures. Finally, Tobias was uncovered and not a moment too soon in the battle he had wandered dangerously close to the edge of the mountain. He now stood only a step away from certain death.

"Now clear my path to the cave," shouted Sabella.

Reluctantly, a path opened up through the mist, creating a walkway up to the cave entrance between a line of lost souls. They all started to edge slowly forwards with Tobias in the lead. The twins were in the middle with the bomb and Sabella brought up the rear still holding up the fireball to keep the body snatchers away who closed in behind them as soon as they had passed.

Reaching the cave entrance, they stepped into the darkness. There was a last angry howl from the souls in the mist and as quickly as they had appeared, they vanished leaving the dark grey clouds circling the mountains once more.

Dropping the fireball to the ground, Sabella turned to the others.

"Is everyone alright?" she asked.

"I think so," replied the twins as they put away their weapons.

"Tobias, are you hurt?" Sabella questioned.

"No, I'm fine," he grumbled. "The only thing that I've hurt is my pride. My job is to look after you and I have failed."

"You haven't failed me in the slightest, you have saved me on more than one occasion and you have guided us here safely.

We will get through this together, whatever lies in our path," said Sabella.

"I just feel like I have let you all down. My job is to protect you."

"You do it well," interrupted Sabella. "You must remember we are in an amazingly complex situation. I am the protector of the orbs and I have been given immense powers to protect all that is living. I need someone to stand by my side and look after me, I'm sorry to say that you have got the task." Sabella smiled.

Looking up at her, a big smile appeared across Tobias' face.

"I cannot think of a place I would rather be young Sabella, I am honoured."

"So please Tobias go back to your grumpy self and tell us what we must do next," she joked.

Walking over to a couple of old torches that were stood up against the wall he bent down and picked them up. He then returned back to the fireball which was still burning on the floor and lit them before handing one to Keltal. Holding his up in front of him the flame flickered and crackled in the wind making eerie shadows dance around them off the black, slimy walls.

"Alright, I will lead the way," Tobias said. "Let's go."

Walking into the blackness it wasn't long before the only light that they had was from the torches they held.

Chapter 18

Slipping and sliding they made their way through the darkness guided by the faint flicker of light being given off by their torches, Sabella used her powers to see through the blackness ahead.

Carefully leading them around rock hazards, and the occasional deep hole which if they had fallen in, they would have disappeared deep into the heart of the mountain. But the most dangerous thing they had to be wary of was the big tentacles of green snotty stuff hanging down from the ceiling. It was dripping acid into the pools on the floor making the rock sizzle and bubble.

Eventually with their flames fading fast they walked the last of the many tight twists and turns, which would have been impossible to navigate at all without the aid of Sabella or their torches. Seeing the sunlight streaming into the tunnel entrance they quickly headed towards it. They stepped out into the open air. Dropping their flames to the ground they looked out over the most amazing view. In front of them swept a very wide set of steps, about a hundred in all, leading down to a mirror like surface. It resembled a giant highly polished ice rink but a hundred times bigger. It was in stark contrast to the black pinnacles of rock that towered above them in a circle like an amphitheatre.

Through some of the gaps in the rocks they could still see the dark grey clouds slowly turning around the outside of the mountain. They stood there for what seemed like an age admiring this amazing place; its calmness, beauty and sense of stillness. It was a shame that this magical place was just a cover for the evil that lay below it.

Breaking the silence Tobias turned to them.

"I think it's time to plant this bomb and head back to the Compton."

Climbing down the steps they all walked out onto the ice. Looking down Sabella found it hard to believe that this highly polished mirror like surface was two miles deep and right at the bottom lay Mortigan entombed for a thousand years in his ice cell, safe guarding the future of every planet, also every living thing.

Lifting his arm up, Tobias looked at his special watch that was helping guide them to the exact spot where the bomb was to be planted. It was showing them that they were getting very close but something wasn't right. The pristine surface that they were crossing was slowly turning to slush. It was like it was melting.

"Is this supposed to be happening?" Sabella asked.

A worried Tobias looked at her. "No something is very wrong."

"So the orbs were right then? There is a dangerous situation with Mortigan?" Sabella exclaimed.

"It looks that way, I can't see any other reason why the ice would be melting unless it was being warmed up. The temperature up here is the same all year 'round, so that can only mean it is being warmed up from below."

A sense of fear suddenly gripped them all. They knew that somehow the evil one was attempting to make his escape.

"We are close, it's just a few more feet," Tobias said.

"Look at that," pointed Sabella.

Stopping Tobias looked at the little red arrows on his watch, then down at the ice. A black swarming mass lay under his feet, moving around within the ice.

"What is it?" Sabella whispered.

But Tobias didn't answer he just kept on staring down. Sabella grabbed hold of his arm and shook it, "What is it?" She asked once more.

"It's very bad," Tobias mumbled. "The bomb isn't going to work; we are too late."

"What do you mean Tobias? Why are we too late and why won't it work?" said Sabella.

"Something has happened deep below us. The bomb was designed to travel two miles down before going off. Whatever we can see is clearly not that far down. Setting the bomb off could mean it detonates too early," replied Tobias.

"What will happen if it does?" she asked.

"We will not be far enough away and we will instantly be killed by its force. It's just too dangerous we will have to head back straightaway. Let's go," Tobias ordered.

Turning, he started to walk off, but Sabella didn't move. She remained there looking deep within the ice at the black mass circling beneath her. Looking back expecting her to be beside him Tobias turned and walked over to her and looked down.

"I'm sorry we failed but for our own safety we really need to leave, right now."

"This is not about us Tobias, it's about the future. My task is to protect everything. If I leave this place now then I have truly failed. If we plant the bomb, then there is still a chance it might put all this right." Sabella still sounding hopeful.

"Yes, but you will die in the process," Tobias said fearful at what she was proposing.

Turning, Sabella looked straight at him.

"If I do, then it was meant to be. I can't leave here without at least trying to put things right. It is my destiny, that you must understand. If you feel you must leave, then I understand. I will stay here to detonate it when you are far enough away."

They all stood there in silence. A warm feeling deep inside of her told her that she was doing the right thing. She was on an incredible journey, new friends had been made, and she had travelled to a far distant planet. One day she was Sabella, just another soul in the sea of millions, now she was Sabella the head sorceress and protector of the same millions. She was far too powerful to decide her own destiny that would be left to the orbs.

Looking up at the sky Tobias sucked in a big gulp of air.

"You're right it is about the protection of so much more, so let's plant the bomb," Tobias said turning to the twins, who were nodding in agreement, they all walked over to the exact spot indicated by the continuing red lights on Tobias' watch. "This is it."

The twins set the box down and opened the lid. Very carefully they lifted the bomb out and gently placed it down on the slushy snow. Just then there was a huge rumble like an earthquake that shook the whole mountain.

"What was that?" asked Sabella alarmingly.

"I wish I knew," replied Tobias. "It came from under the ice. It is getting a lot darker under our feet by the second. We need to go so let's hurry, press the button and run for our lives."

Standing around the bomb Tobias looked at Keltal and Kaylum.

"You two have carried the bomb here safely so I would like you both to press the button."

Leaning down the twins reached for the button simultaneously but before they could press it there was a loud cracking sound and large splits started to appear in the ice. There was a rumbling sound, a high pitch hissing sound could be heard as the air was escaping from the broken ice. Black smoke and ash shot up into the air. First in one place and then another. It poured from the ice with such force it sounded like a jet plane flying over their heads.

"Press the button," yelled Tobias.

Together the twins pushed the big red button on the bomb and there was a buzzing sound, instantly the bomb started to heat up. Within seconds it was glowing red and slowly starting to sink beneath the ice. With more explosions, cracks and columns of black smoke appearing around them it was time to run.

Taking off they ran for the safety of the steps which would take them back up to the tunnel.

"Don't look back," shouted Tobias. "Just keep running."

But it was very hard to run when the whole mountain seemed to be moving and time and time again it shook with such force that they were thrown to the ground. But it was one in particular movement that scared them the most. The whole ice field rose up some three meters or more. Something massive had exploded deep beneath them causing them to be thrown through the air before crashing to the ground and sliding to a stop.

Sabella looked back to where they had planted the bomb to see the whole ice field imploding in on itself. Everything was disappearing into a black smoking hole and it was spreading quickly outwards towards them. She then felt someone grab her from behind and lift her to her feet.

"Run," shouted Tobias.

Taking off once more Sabella ran as fast as her tired legs would carry her. Sheer panic helped, and the fact that everything was disappearing into a two-mile deep hole full of fire behind her.

Eventually, they all reached the steps which led up to the tunnel, by now her legs were burning so each step felt like she was lifting a block of lead. Progress was painfully slow and was hindered by the fact the steps were crumbling away beneath them. Scrambling to the top she turned around to see Tobias falling backwards. Reaching out his arm he managed to grab hold of one of the broken edges of step and now hung there in mid-air as the ground slipped away into the abyss below him.

"Keltal, Kaylum help Tobias," Sabella shouted.

Holding on to each other the twins stretched out to Tobias who in turn reached out with his free hand. After many attempts, they managed to lock fingers and not a moment too soon as the remaining steps fell away and he was left swinging freely in mid-air held only by the twins. As they pulled him to safety he glanced down into the fiery depths. It was then that he noticed something moving. Black shapes were crawling up the wall towards him. He couldn't make out what they were until they got closer.

"Vipers," Tobias whispered. "Hurry we need to go we have company."

"What did you see?" asked Sabella.

"Viper warriors, thousands of them climbing up the walls towards us."

"But what about the sunlight, won't that stop them?"

"I don't know, Sabella, maybe the black smoke is blocking the sun's rays or maybe they have evolved. Anyway we are not waiting around to find out, it's time to move, now."

Making their way into the tunnel which would take them to the other side of the mountain, away from the evil that was bearing down on them, it soon became clear that it was not going to be that easy, as the mountain shook, trembling under the tremendous explosions that were taking place deep below them. The tunnel was collapsing.

Large chunks of rock were falling from the walls and roof, kicking up big clouds of dust which was going to make their task of getting to the other side even harder. It could even collapse, completely burying them in the mountain forever. But it was their only way out and they had to take the risk. Edging forward into darkness it soon became apparent it was going to be harder than ever, they just couldn't see what was in front of them.

"Stop," shouted Tobias, over the creaking and moaning of the mountain. "This is impossible. One of us is going to be killed."

"But we can't go back," Keltal replied. "You have seen the army of warriors coming towards us, there is no way we can fight that many."

"Keltal is right," shouted Sabella, "Going back would be suicide we have to carry on this way through the tunnel. If I generate a fireball to give us a light, the twins shelter us with their mechanical arms there may be a chance we can get to the other side. I think it's our only option."

"Okay we have to try," agreed Tobias.

Holding her hands out in front of her Sabella generated a burning orb in the palms of her hands giving them light. The twins then put up their massive metal arms to shield them and they set off once more into the dust and darkness, the deep rumbling echoes surrounding them.

Chapter 19

Fighting their way through the crumbling remains of the tunnel, dodging falling rocks, and walking through choking clouds of dust, they eventually made it to a point where they could see light at the end of the tunnel. It was a welcomed sight and a vast contrast from the devastation they had left behind, the mist had now descended at the end of the tunnel, making visibility very difficult.

It was then that Sabella heard a distant spine-chilling roar, which made her spin around and look into the darkness. It was a noise she had heard before, one that would only mean danger and imminent attack. It was the sound of a viper warrior but not one, this was thousands and it was getting louder. The ground beneath their feet was beginning to shudder.

"Tobias," Sabella shouted out.

"I can hear them," Tobias replied.

"What are we going to do?" Sabella asked.

"We're going to jump," Tobias explained. "In the back of our coats the Professor has built in some sort of parachute for emergency cases. Sabella you need to run and throw yourself off the mountain, when clear you pull the cord to deploy the shoot. You will float to the ground where you can unclip it, and leave it behind."

"You are saying that we are to run out of the tunnel, off the edge of the mountain and hope that a makeshift shoot pops out of the back of our coats that will take us safely to the ground? Can you hear what you are saying?" said Sabella.

"Have you any reason not to trust the Professor and his inventions?" asked Tobias.

"No not at all," Sabella replied. "I am scared it is a leap of faith."

"Yes, Sabella, but it is the only choice we have apart from staying and fighting. You have seen how many warriors are coming towards us. You might be able to hold them off for a while but not forever. I will be honest with you and tell you that we are out of options. They will be here in moments, so I suggest that Keltal go first, Kaylum you will guard us from behind until Sabella and I are safe from the mountain, then come yourself."

Keltal got himself ready and with a nod from Tobias he started to run up the tunnel. Once he was clear of the cave he vanished into the mist. The remaining three stood there in silence for a while not knowing what had happened to him.

"Do you think he made it?" Sabella asked.

"We won't know that yet," replied Tobias. "Until we have made the jump ourselves. You go next, Sabella, I will follow you."

"Surely with my fire power it would be better for me to stay here with Kaylum. Then I will follow you?" Sabella said.

"No, no this will go against everything, remember I am your protector, I will not leave you behind," said Tobias.

"But it doesn't matter if I go first or second Tobias, the point is I will have to do it alone," said Sabella.

Just then a loud roar echoed through the cave as the first of the warriors came running out of the darkness.

"They are here, go now," shouted Kaylum as he swung his sword and struck the warrior destroying it immediately.

Soon many more were coming towards them.

"You need to go Tobias," shouted Sabella.

"I can't leave you behind," Tobias yelled back over the noise which echoed off the walls.

"You have to, all three of us can't go at the same time, if you and I go then Kaylum will be overwhelmed and killed. I need to stay and help keep the warriors at bay now please go, we will follow as soon as you are clear."

Standing next to Kaylum and remembering her time training in the room with Marmaduke she unleashed her full firepower shooting bolts of burning flames out the palms of her hands destroying multiple viper warriors as they ran towards them with weapons drawn, mouths open with hate. Looking over her shoulder Sabella saw Tobias ready himself. Holding the cord in his hand he looked back over his shoulder at her and with sadness at leaving her behind, he started running.

Reaching the end of the tunnel he vanished into the mist and was gone.

The number of warriors now attacking them was vast; they were slowly being pushed backwards. There was a rumbling within the mountain which shook the ground beneath their feet. Clouds of dust bellowed up the tunnel towards them.

"The tunnel is going to give way any minute," Sabella shouted. "I will create a wall of fire, when I have that is when we will run."

"Alright," shouted Kaylum back as he swung his sword wildly destroying another batch of warriors.

Holding the palms of her hands up Sabella slowly brought them together creating a curtain of flames across the tunnel from wall to wall which crackled and crept across the roof. Although it stopped the warriors from getting to them it didn't stop them from attacking, again and again they jumped into the flames before instantly turning into ash as they did so, their weapons falling to the ground and piling up around their feet. Even though there was no way through the flames some were still willing to sacrifice themselves whilst others started to throw their weapons through the curtain of flames. Spears, shields and swords were now flying at them, some were ricocheting off the walls narrowly missing them as they backed up towards the tunnels entrance.

"We need to go now," shouted Kaylum over the deafening roar of warriors and metal on rock.

"Let's do it," Sabella shouted back as she reached up and unzipped the pouch behind her head, which hopefully contained the parachute and took hold of the pull cord which would hopefully deploy it. Looking at Kaylum there was no need for words as she knew they were both scared stiff and knew they had to make the jump. Staying where they were was no longer an option, the wall of flames was now being breached due to the sheer number of warriors pushing towards them. Sabella and Kaylum started running up the last bit of tunnel, with warriors chasing them they disappeared into the mist.

They were instantly separated as their coats were tugged back by the dead souls but they had to keep going. Blinded by the mist, with warriors roaring in anger a few feet behind them they ran for their lives, towards the edge of the mountain. It was then that the ground beneath Sabella's feet shook violently and disappeared. Flying she held the parachute cord tightly in her hand, once clear of the mountain she would pull it. She had never felt fear like it before. Open air and freedom didn't come, instead she hit the ground hard and started to slide and tumble down the mountainside. She no longer had hold of the pull cord. If she fell off the edge now it spelled disaster for her. Clearing the mist and in desperation to stop herself falling any further she threw her arms out and grabbed hold of a rock, her legs swinging around beneath her off the edge of the mountain.

Luckily, the rock held she now hung thousands of feet in the air. With everything crumbling, shaking around her Sabella held on by her fingertips, she looked down and watched falling rocks disappearing into the abyss below.

"Sabella," came a shout from behind her.

Looking around she saw Kaylum who was floating with his parachute open, "Sabella look you have to jump," Kaylum shouted again.

"I can't," Sabella called back in desperation.

"No, look up," he urged pointing frantically.

Lifting her head up she looked into the eyes of a viper warrior who was lifting his weapon up above his head, roaring loudly before taking a swing at her.

Letting go of the rock, Sabella pushed herself backwards and began to fall as the warrior's sword hit the rocks sending sparks flying. With arms and legs flailing the black rock fell past her eyes and the wind roared in her ears. Everything was a blur she couldn't make out the ground from the sky as she hurtled towards the foot of the mountain. Desperately she tried again and again to grab hold of the cord to her pull shoot as it flapped around in the wind. Finally grabbing it she pulled it as hard as she could.

There was a slight delay before she was yanked upwards by the force of the wind filling the shoot. Floating away from the mountain she looked down. Far below her she could see two little dots which were Keltal and Tobias. Just above her Kaylum drifted along on the same breeze waving and shouting at her although she couldn't hear what he was saying, by his actions he looked happy to see her safe. As she slowly descended to Earth, she looked back to the mountain. It was obvious something had gone badly wrong, black smoke now bellowed high into the sky from deep within the crater. It was now so vast that it was blocking the sun creating long shadows. Within these shadows walked a new breed of warrior, one that could walk in daylight though still not in direct sunlight. Mortigan had not been dormant for all these years he had been evolving his army and planning his escape back out into the world, now this army stood on the mountain top in their thousands. Bigger and stronger than ever, a new threat had been created and daylight was no longer a deterrent or safe time of the day.

Chapter 20

Floating gently to the ground, Sabella sunk into the snow up to her waist, immediately she noticed the temperature had dropped dramatically.

"I'm so glad you're safe, Sabella," said Tobias relieved.

"I'm not sure we will all be safe for long," Sabella replied.

"What do you mean?" Tobias asked.

"Haven't you noticed anything different with the warriors?" Sabella said. "They have evolved, they can walk in daylight and are coming our way. Look," she said pointing up at the mountain, they move so fast.

It was now alive with warriors swarming down towards them.

"That's impossible," said Tobias. "No warrior has ever been able to stand daylight."

"Well they can now, they walk within the shadows. If that black cloud casts its shadow over us then it means they can get to us. While there is sunlight between us, we have a chance to make it back to the Compton, but we need to go now," Sabella explained.

"Kaylum, Keltal," ordered Tobias, helping Sabella up and unclipping her parachute. "Put on your snow shoes, we need to move fast, don't look back."

As fast as they could they all took off across the ice field trying their hardest to put some distance between themselves and the fast-moving warriors. All the time the cloud was creeping up on them, but the deep, powdery snow was sapping their strength and hindering their progress. Eventually, they reached the hill which took them from the flat plain up to the ice curve.

Stopping to catch her breath Sabella took a quick look over her shoulder. The clouds shadow had caught them up and was now right upon them. Being so fast and agile the warriors had made up large amounts of ground. They could cover distances very quickly, even if it was soft snow. As the shadow finally crept up to her feet she looked up at the mountain. Thick black smoke was still coming from its depths.

"Sabella don't stop we need to keep moving," called Tobias hurrying over to her.

Looking across the once pure white plain, it was now a creeping mass of black ant like creatures. Which were now so close you could hear their roar.

"We're not going to make it, are we?" Sabella asked.

"I'm afraid not," replied Tobias in a soft voice. Lifting his arm, he looked at the special watch given to him by the Professor.

"I don't believe there is any point in looking at this, as I don't think it is going to detonate after all. Whatever Mortigan has done has made the bomb useless even if we did achieve our first goal of planting it. But sadly, it seems we were far too late for he was obviously ahead of us and has been planning his escape for many years. The sad thing is he will now be free to roam the universe and wreak havoc at will."

With sadness Sabella looked at him, "I wish I had known about my powers years ago, I feel I belong with you and the others at castle cove, I was just starting to settle into my new life. I'm just sad that I will never get the chance to fulfil my destiny I have a deep fear of what will become of everyone and everything if I am not there to protect them."

"That Sabella I'm afraid is out of your hands. Darkness now has the upper hand, the battle between good and evil has always raged since the dawn of time. Maybe it is time for a change, but whatever happens then sadly we won't be around to witness it. For us our journey is over so in our last stand let us take out as many of these creatures as possible and give good a chance over evil."

Viper warriors had now circled them all for as far as the eye could see. It was a black moving mass of evil, still more were coming down the mountainside. Standing back to back with the twins Tobias and Sabella looked at each other for the last time. She may have been about to die at the hands of Mortigan's evil army but she would be doing so with her most loyal of friends who themselves were willing to lay down their lives for her and the fight against evil. It was with deep sadness that she wouldn't be fulfilling her new duty as sorceress, nor exploring her new home, most of all not knowing the fate of her mother at the hands of the chameleon warrior. It was with that thought that she stared into a thousand lifeless black eyes which were moving ever closer, stamping their feet and weapons together in time and making a strange haunting sound, chanting together. Building the fire up inside her stomach she was determined to take out as many as possible before they were all over whelmed. Holding her hands up with her palms pointing outwards she took aim, but before she could fire there was a sudden shaking under her feet, a distant rumble which sounded as though it was coming from the heart of the island.

"Look," shouted Tobias pointing at the mountain. The thick black cloud which had been rising from its fiery depths had gone, all that was left were a couple of wispy white streams creeping into the sky.

"What's happened, Tobias?" Sabella shouted over the roar of the warriors who after being stopped in their tracks briefly were now resuming their chant and moving ever closer.

"It's the bomb it's detonated," he yelled back. "We've done it but sadly we won't get to celebrate our triumph for in less than a moment the thousands of warriors that are stood before us and every living thing on this island will be frozen solid forever and that includes us."

"Can't we get into the tents?" asked Sabella.

"There's no time Sabella, look," Tobias replied pointing towards the mountain.

She could see a giant wave of ice coming down its sides. It was moving incredibly fast, within a few seconds it had reached the bottom and started spreading out, rolling across the snowy plain. It's thunderous echo getting ever louder as it sped towards them like a tsunami.

She could see the wall of death engulfing the warriors, in the next few seconds it would be upon them, freezing them instantly where they stood.

With a raging fire built up inside of her she looked at her hands. Just under the skin she could see a red glow of power which she was intending to use on the warriors. An idea then came to her.

"Tobias," she shouted over the ever-increasing noise. "Take my tent from my rucksack."

"But we have no time," he answered.

"Please just do it," Sabella ordered pointing the palm of her hands downwards at the grounds she blasted off a stream of fire bolts which instantly melted the ice in front of her creating a hole. She kept going until it was just big enough for them all to fit into.

"Everybody get in," Sabella cried as one by one they all dived into it and sat tightly together, putting the tent over the top of them tucking it all in around the sides, preparing for what was about to happen.

First came the noise, it was like a jet plane flying low over their heads and it suddenly became very dark as the blast screamed passed over the top of them. But worst of all was the cold. The tent that was covering them froze solid, it became extremely hard to breathe ice crystals instantly formed covering them. Penetrating their coats, the pain was so much that they cried out in agony as the ice attacked their bodies and tried to freeze them to the bone.

As quickly as it had come it disappeared across the island on its devastating path of destruction. Sunlight now flooded back into the hole and Sabella struggled to open her eyes. She was covered in a thick layer of ice. As she moved it cracked and fell away in big chunks. Slowly, the twins stretched and stood up. As they did, the tent crumbled into dust. With icicles hanging from his beard Tobias turned and looked at Sabella. "Thank you, Sabella you saved our lives."

"I was just using the skills I have to protect us all. We have saved each other since we first set out on our journey. We need to get out of here, I pushed my heat button in my coat but it's having no effect I'm freezing so it's time for us to get back to the Compton. We have achieved our goal so it's now time to go home to Castle Cove."

Climbing out of their ice hole they surveyed their new surroundings. For as far as their eyes could see all the way back to the foot of the mountain a whole army of warriors stood encased in ice, thousands of them just glistening in the sunlight. Even the ground they were now stood on was half a metre thick with the clearest ice, and as the sun shone, they looked like they were walking on water. It was also as flat as glass making walking become skating on ice.

Setting off for the Compton there was a possibility it may not have survived the power of the ice bomb. Both Keltal and Kaylum led the way, weapons drawn out they smashed a path through the sea of frozen warriors. Chunks of ice flew into the air as they ploughed their way forward. Eventually, they reached open land and with a final look back at the now peaceful mountain, in the distance they made their way up to the ice scoop, hopefully on to the safety of the Compton.

Chapter 21

Feeling a lot warmer, Sabella climbed and scrambled her way up towards the ice scoop sweeping up high overhead. The sun was beaming through the clear ice which was casting rainbow coloured patterns that slowly moved across the floor. All of them were now happy at fulfilling their task and entombing Mortigan for another thousand years.

They hoped the journey back to the Compton would be quick and trouble free. However, in an unpredictable place like nothing Sabella had ever known before things could change in an instant. A deep rumbling sound made them turn and look up at the mountain.

"What was that?" asked Sabella looking up at the summit for signs of movement.

Tobias didn't look at her but instead focused his gaze out across the white landscape.

"I don't know," Tobias said slowly. "Whatever it was it has stopped now. Maybe it's just the island settling after the bomb. Let's carry on back to the Compton; I'd rather not wait any longer."

As they embarked upon their return journey they were instantly thrown to the ground by an almighty explosion. It felt so big like the whole island had been lifted up and dropped back down. Smoke erupted once more from within the heart of the mountain and a black mass of warriors poured over the top.

"Look Sabella," said Tobias. "Oh no, I don't understand, more warriors," Tobias said pointing at the black river streaming down towards them once more.

"They are moving fast so we need to go," Sabella replied as she staggered to her feet only to be thrown down once more by a second bigger explosion.

Fire, rocks and ash shot high into the sky, so big was the eruption that cracks started appearing in the ice scoop. Bits started to fall off the top, shards of razor-sharp ice crashed down around them. To make matters worse a third deeper sound rumbled and vibrated beneath them. The snowy white flat plain that they had walked across to the foot of the mountain opened up in a rage of fire and steam. Black water bubbled from its depths as the island started to break apart.

"Keltal, Kaylum protect Sabella, do whatever it takes," ordered Tobias.

Getting up they stumbled over to where Sabella was having great difficulty staying on her feet with the island vibrating so violently. Shielding her with Tobias they made their way through the crumbling ice curve, taking many hits from falling debris as it crashed down on top of them. Finally, they reached the end and not a moment too soon as thousands of tons of ice plummeted to the ground. There was no time to reflect on their near miss, the island was imploding in on itself and warriors were once again closing in on them.

The next obstacle in front of them was to make it safely down the long steep slope that led to the great expanse of field ice. It would lead them from the islands edge all the way out to the Compton which sat deep in sea mist somewhere in the far distance. The only way they were going to be able to find it was with the watch Tobias had around his wrist.

"Behind us," shouted one of the twins pointing to a large crack opening up and coming their way.

Moving backward it got to a point where they had no choice but to descend the slippery slope. Instantly, Keltal lost his footing and his sheer size and weight dragged the rest of them over the edge and down. Sliding on their backs, picking up speed, they were totally out of control. The four of them sped towards the foot of the slope, unable to stop or control which direction they were heading. Blinded by the snow which was flying up into her face Sabella couldn't make out anything in front of her, except to her left she could just see Tobias speeding past in a cloud of white dust. He had taken a tumble and was now zooming past her with his arms out stretched in front of him like he was flying.

The twins due to their bulk were now a long way in front. Tobias disappeared into the ground vanishing. Time and time again Sabella shouted his name but there was no answer. As she neared the bottom of the slope from what seemed like a hundred miles an hour, she careered into a massive snow bank up to her neck, sending a cloud of snow up into the air.

Regaining her senses, she looked up into the sky and saw the twins looking back at her. Grabbing an arm each, they pulled her out from the snow bank.

"Tobias, we have lost Tobias," Sabella said panicking. "We need to find him."

They all looked back up the slope for any sign of life. It was then that a puff of snow appeared to be coming from a large hole in the ground. It could be the island breaking up but within seconds a screaming Tobias shot out high into the air, his arms and legs flailing around. Over their heads he flew and disappeared into the same snow bank that Sabella had crashed into. The three of them dived in after him and dug with their hands. Uncovering his face Sabella looked down at him.

"Tobias are you alright, are you hurt?"

Giving a big cough he opened his eyes. "I'm a bit winded but in one piece, I think. Can you help me up?"

Grabbing his hands, they pulled him free from the snow. A little bit shaky he dusted himself down.

"Are you sure you are alright?" Sabella asked again, "That was a big fall, you had us all worried."

"Apart from my leg hurting a bit I think I got off pretty lightly. Anyway, there is no time to dwell on it as the warriors are closing in and the island is sinking," said Tobias.

It was now clearly visible that the land mass had broken away from the floating field ice they were stood on, it was sinking beneath the sea. The mountain in the far distance was now a mass of fire and smoke with big veins of lava running down its sides. Fishers had opened up everywhere spurting black sooty water but still the warriors kept coming. They had now reached the top of the slope, at the speed they were moving it wouldn't be long before they were able to attack them once more.

"Move," ordered Tobias.

Setting off across the frozen ice field, it was gently moving up and down as the island sunk deeper into the abyss. It soon became clear that Tobias had injured his leg badly and he was struggling to walk let alone run. Even if Tobias hadn't injured his leg, they wouldn't make it back to the Compton. In the shadow from the smoke of the mountain the warriors were gaining in on them once more.

As they carried on, they came across the sledges which were still encased in ice. Tobias slumped to the ground. They were all exhausted and had not had food or rest since they headed up the mountain. There certainly wasn't going to be time now. In the distance the warriors were numbering in their thousands. Reaching the bottom of the slope they all climbed from the sinking island onto the ice field.

This really was going to be their last stand. They couldn't see a way they were going to make it back to the ship. Here on the frozen wasteland was going to be their final battle. The twins lifted Tobias to his feet and they all drew their weapons and waited for the inevitable. Enraged with anger at escaping the warriors the first time around, Sabella climbed up onto the engine of the sledge to get a better angle of attack, so she could unleash her firepower. Everything she had learnt had brought her too this moment. Summoning every last ounce of energy, she created a power within in her so intense that the ice that had formed on her coat was melting away, where it was actually starting to steam.

Looking down at her feet she noticed the ice underneath and around them had also melted away.

"Just maybe," Sabella whispered. "Tobias, I have an idea."

"We don't need an idea, Sabella, we need a miracle."

"Well I might have one of them," Sabella called over the noise of the advancing army. "Look."

Turning around, Tobias looked to where she was pointing.

"If I melt the ice on the engine do you think it will start?"

"At a guess I would say yes," Tobias replied. "But you only have a minute or so."

Jumping down she tore off her gloves and placed her hands directly onto the engine. Instantly, the ice encasing it started to melt. Dripping to begin with, but before long water was running off of it.

"I will keep going, you try to start it," Sabella said to Tobias.

Flicking a lever and turning a knob he took hold of the pull cord and gave it a massive tug. The engine turned over which was good news but wouldn't start. Again and again he pulled but nothing happened.

"Start," Tobias shouted. "Will you start?"

"They are nearly here," called Kaylum. "It's too late we are going to have to fight."

"It will start," he mumbled to himself flicking another switch. "Maybe it's too warm so I don't need the choke on." Taking the pull cord one last time he gave it an almighty pull. There was a little splutter as the engine roared into life, not a moment too soon as the warriors were now in range and the first of their arrows were dropping close to them.

"Quick all on," Tobias shouted.

Climbing on board, Tobias gave the little engine maximum power. Turning it around, they powered across the ice away from the warriors at such a speed. The warriors lunged for the sledge, grabbing hold they fish tailed behind them growling and hissing. They held on with one hand and waved their weapons with the other.

Drawing their swords, the twins soon dispatched them in a now familiar puff of dust, their spears bounced and rolled across the ice. Now clear of the evil army they just had to hope and pray that there was enough fuel to see them back to the Compton and that the little engine held together. With four people on board, it was having to work extremely hard on maximum power. Going any slower just wasn't an option. The warriors could run so fast that the sledge was only just making ground on them. The smallest little hiccup or mistake could spell disaster, even when they reached the Compton they wouldn't have long to get on board and out into open water. The main thing was after all their encounters with death and destruction they were still alive and fighting. Getting back to the Compton was now critical for them and that of everyone on every living planet. The first important part, all hinged on a little tiny smoking engine that was pulling them across the ice field.

Chapter 22

Time and distance seemed to be moving very slowly since their last encounter with the viper warriors. They all knew the many thousands of evil relentless killing machines were not too far behind them, tracking them by scent and sound, like a pack of wild dogs.

The thick mist which had descended was camouflaging them a little but it was also hindering their safe passage to the Compton. It made it extremely hard to see what was in front of them because of the white out. Occasionally, the sledge would fly into the air or shoot down a hollow at any moment they could be sent crashing out of control and soon back into the clutches of the chasing warriors.

It was a heart stopping moment when they thought they were going to disappear right through the ice after just having flown over a small snow bank, crashing down into a large pool of ice and water which washed over them with such force they nearly came to a complete stop.

Tobias kept the throttle wide open and they crept through, the poor little engine was now suffering as black smoke began belching from the exhaust and there was a bad misfire. It wasn't going to be long before the whole thing seized solid and died.

"Keep your eyes peeled," Tobias shouted over his shoulder as he looked at his watch. "We are very close."

"Over there," shouted Kaylum. "There's something black in the mist."

Coming around to the left, Tobias pointed them towards the big black figure which was starting to appear out of the gloom.

"It's the Compton," they all shouted in celebration as the ship came into view.

The little engine gave one last cough and came to a stop. Climbing off the sledge they all staggered the last two hundred meters to the side of the ship. The twins helped Tobias along as his injury seemed to have worsened.

It was a little silvery robot who met them first.

"Captain, Sabella, Kaylum and Keltal you made it. We feared the worst when we saw the explosions and heard the distant rumbles, but you are here now, and you're safe. Hold on, I will drop the rope ladder," said Paiter as he lifted it up over the side and lowered it down to them.

By the time Tobias had struggled to the top, the Professor was there to greet them.

"Captain, you're injured," Professor Brumbles squealed, helping Tobias over the side rail.

"Don't worry about me, Professor, you can patch me up later. Is the ship ready for sail, Paiter?"

"It is captain but at the moment we are stuck in the field ice. All attempts to free her up to now have failed. Unfortunately, the ice bomb froze us in solid."

"Damn," Tobias muttered under his breath, "Professor, is the sunlight beam and shield operational yet?"

"Unfortunately no, Captain. They froze when the freeze bomb hit us, a couple more hours and it will be as good as new," answered the Professor.

Suddenly, shouting could be heard from down on the ice.

"They are here," called one of the twins.

"Who are?" asked the Professor leaning over the side.

"The warriors," pointed Kaylum.

Peering out into the icy mist, the Professor watched the advancing black mass coming into view. Stumbling back open-mouthed, he stared at the army of thousands.

"They are in daylight," Professor Brumbles stammered.

"Yes, Professor, they are. Now listen," ordered Tobias. "I need you to concentrate. I need you to get the sunlight beam, and shield up and running, I don't need to tell you that you don't have a few hours. You only have a matter of minutes."

"Yes," nodded the Professor as he scurried off.

"Paiter," called Tobias.

"Yes, Captain?"

"I need you to get us out of this ice. Give her full power, do whatever it takes to free us. We will give you as much time as we can."

"Okay, Captain," replied Paiter, heading off to the wheelhouse.

Leaning over the side Tobias looked down to see Sabella nearing the top of the rope ladder. The twins were still down on the ice with weapons drawn preparing to take on the thousands single-handedly in the protection of the ship.

"Kaylum, Keltal come on board," Tobias shouted down to them.

Hearing him shout the twins climbed the rope ladder and over the side rail as the first of the arrows bounced off the side of the metal hull.

"Kaylum, Keltal," ordered Tobias. "I need you to guard the port and starboard sides. I will take the stern, Sabella you can take the bow. Let's keep them at bay for as long as possible, and hope the Professor can get the security systems working and Paiter can get us out of here. Right, let's get to our stations, do all you can, good luck to us all." Looking at Sabella he gave her a half-smile. "Be careful," Tobias mouthed.

"You too," Sabella whispered back before turning and running across the deck.

Arrows were now raining down onto the ship; staying low she crept forward until she reached the bow. Slowly, she peered over the side. The landscape had totally changed in colour from white to black for as far as the eye could see. Disappearing into the mist was now a sea of angry raging warriors. But not only in one direction, they had completely surrounded the Compton and were now closing in for the kill.

Ducking back down, Sabella closed her eyes and summoned up her power. Preparing herself she quickly jumped up and fired off two fire bolts, one out of each hand. So powerful were her abilities that they cut two swathes in the warriors, instantly vaporising hundreds in a single shot. All that were left were two massive white lines of snow. She ducked back down and recharged once more. Looking down the deck she could see that warriors had now made it on board. The twins and Tobias were doing their best to hold them back but it was only a matter of time before they had complete control over the Compton. Jumping up once more she unleashed another barrage of fire bolts.

The warriors were now up against the ship she could hear their spears ricocheting off the hull. Looking up she noticed a black cloud arching over the top of the warriors like a massive flock of birds. Thousands heading towards the ship with a screeching noise accompanying them. As the black mass started to dip down towards the Compton, it became clear that these were no birds, it was in fact arrows. Diving down she tucked herself into the side of the ship. The screeching noise increased until the arrows hit. Sabella couldn't see Tobias as he was behind the wheelhouse, but by the state of the twins who had arrows sticking out of them, staggering around injured but still courageously fighting on Tobias must have been badly injured for he was nowhere near as strong as the twins. It was over, they had lost the battle and they were on the verge of losing the war.

Jumping up for a final time Sabella looked down the deck of the Compton and unleashed her full firepower. Warriors were instantly turned to ash as she stood her ground and fired in all directions. Even when a warrior jumped onto the deck behind her and stuck his spear into her shoulder, she spun around and vaporised it. She could feel the poison now coursing through her body but she didn't stop, instead she intensified her attack, blasting warriors off the deck.

It was then in the distance she noticed the ice ripping apart, opening up accompanied by a deep thundering cracking sound. She had a feeling, a sense, what was heading towards the ship.

"Mortigan," Sabella shouted. Forgetting the warriors, she focused her power on the evil crashing through the ice just under the surface. Fireballs rained down on the dark shadow, Sabella's nemesis.

Suddenly, an arrow dug deep into her leg then one in her arm. Staggering backwards she reeled in pain as a final arrow hit her in the chest but she was going to fight till the last. Her archenemy was only metres away now. Pushing the ice ahead of him like a bulldozer pushes earth. Warriors were being thrown to the side as he headed for the ship. In her final act of defiance Sabella put her hands together, summoning her last ounce of power. Just as he was about to hit, she fired a huge fire bolt which struck the ice and exploded. At the same time the sunlight beam shone out instantly cutting down every warrior that stood on the ice. Exhausted and in tremendous pain Sabella stumbled and dropped to her knees without an ounce of energy left rolled onto her side. Things were gradually becoming hazy, she could still see the twins and hear the noise but all was becoming dark. She no longer had the strength to keep her eyes open and as they shut, she drifted to another place.

Chapter 23

The Compton quietly rocked from side to side. Now free from the ice and it's vice like grip, every last warrior had been destroyed. Calm and tranquillity had returned to the ship. Only the distant rumble and the faint orange glow through the mist was all that remained of the island as it disappeared beneath the waves. Shouts of joy rang out from various parts of the ship, but for one little robot he knelt down beside the body of his mistress with overpowering sadness and pain.

Hobbling from behind the wheelhouse calling her name Tobias' face dropped at seeing Sabella's body on the deck of the Compton Jester trying to gently wake her. As fast as he could he made his way up to her, kneeling down he opened her coat. Her injuries were clear; part of a poison arrow could still be seen sticking from her chest with so much blood.

"Sabella, can you hear me? Sabella, it's Tobias," he called out.

"Sir, is Miss Sabella going to be alright?" Jester asked.

"I don't know my little friend. I just don't know," Tobias replied, his voice breaking. "Twins go straight downstairs and prepare the Professor. I will bring Sabella down."

Gently scooping her up he staggered across the deck to the doorway with Jester loyally carrying her sword and following on behind. Stepping through the doorway, he descended the stairs to where the twins and the Professor were waiting. As he reached the bottom, a strange noise started up, like the buzzing of electricity. Then before their eyes, the strangest thing started to happen. First one by one, each of the pillars in the corridor lit up brightly. Then in the middle of the corridor the walls started to move backwards until they had formed a circle in the middle of the ship.

"Professor, what's happening?" Tobias asked.

"I don't know, Captain," replied the Professor.

"What do you mean you don't know? You built it," Tobias was agitated.

"Well," the Professor paused. "I did, and I didn't."

It was then, that in the middle of the floor, in the centre of the circle rose, four ghostly figures appeared with a blue aura around them. A heat haze drifted off them, their eyes looked like balls of electricity. Turning towards them, they glided across the floor; sparks flew off of them as they moved. Drawing their weapons, the twins stood in protection of Sabella and the others. Reaching out one of the strange apparitions touched Keltal's sword, instantly melting it down to the handle. Burning his hand Keltal dropped it to the floor.

"Keltal, Kaylum step aside," Tobias ordered.

Doing as they were told, the twins stepped back. Moving forward the four strangers now stood in front of Tobias who was still holding Sabella in his arms. Holding her up, Tobias offered the lifeless body to the ghosts.

"Captain, what are you doing?" asked the Professor. "They might be evil, something to do with Mortigan."

"Somehow I don't think so. Do you?" Tobias replied. "What other options do we have? As far as we know she might already be dead."

Holding his arms outstretched they watched as Sabella's body rose into the air. Slowly, she drifted across the room and hovered in the middle of the circle. Every single pillar in the corridor then started to pulse, gradually getting faster until the light looked continuous. Moving out to the edge of the circle at equal distances the ghostly strangers focused on Sabella. The whirling noise that they had heard when they come down the stairs into the ship slowly faded. It was replaced with a massive cracking sound of electricity as lightning shot from the chests of the entities. It passed through the air across the circle in all four directions, connecting with Sabella's body in the middle. She now floated, suspended in a ball of energy.

"Captain, what's happening now?" asked Jester.

"I don't know," Tobias replied. "We just have to wait. Whatever is occurring is far advanced of any of us and what we know. Whoever or whatever these things are they must know what they are doing. It's like they were waiting for Sabella and they know who she is. Only time will tell. Our job is to get her home safely, she is on the ship and there is a lot of work to be done. It is a potentially dangerous journey ahead of us, we need to get the Compton ship shape, to be able to get Sabella home to Castle Cove. Jester, can you assist Paiter in the wheelhouse for the time being? I'm going to stay with Sabella, but I will inform you of any changes in her condition."

"Thank you, Captain," replied the little robot.

Tobias then turned to Kaylum and Keltal. "You two have been a tower of strength, shown amazing courage and bravery. It hasn't gone unnoticed with me or Sabella we are truly grateful. I can see you are both in pain and injured, go with the Professor to his quarters and get fixed up before either of you do anything else."

"What about you, Captain?" asked Keltal. "You don't look too good yourself."

"I'm alright, I need to stay here with Sabella, anyway the Professor and I have a lot to talk about. Isn't that right, Mr Brumbles?" Tobias said rather sharply.

"I guess so," he replied sheepishly before ushering the twins down the corridor to his quarters and shutting the door behind them.

Sliding down the wall Tobias sat there staring at the four ghostly figures, with the big arcs of lightning keeping Sabella suspended in the middle of the circle, encased in a ball of electricity. Who were they? Where did they come from? What were they doing to Sabella? It was obvious the Professor didn't have a clue, but he did have a lot of questions to answer. Maybe Sabella was onto something when she questioned the engine room, and the Professor's skill in building something so complex.

Once the twins were patched up, the Professor would be able to start answering some of the questions.

Resting his head against one of the pillars, exhausted he fell asleep.

Up on deck the two little robots were doing a great job of navigating the Compton out the ice, back through to the open water. Paiter was at the helm guiding the ship, Jester was attacking the big job of clearing the deck of arrows and spears left behind by the warriors. The Compton was in pretty good shape considering what she had been through. Slowly, turning the ship gently eased forward using the paddles. She split the ice with the bow cutter that was still deployed at the front.

Waking with a jolt Tobias sat up he gradually opened his eyes. The light from the lightning bolts shooting across to Sabella's body were so bright he squinted before slowly focusing his eyes on his surroundings. He noticed the twins were sat across from him. "How long have I been asleep?" Tobias asked.

"Hours, Captain," answered the twins together.

"Really?" Tobias muttered. "Has anything happened yet?" he said looking at Sabella.

"Nothing has changed," explained Keltal. "It's still the same you haven't missed anything. Well nothing we can see," he added.

"How are you both?" Tobias asked. "Did the Professor fix you up?"

"Yes, Captain," the twins replied. "We are as good as new and ready for work."

"That's good," Tobias replied as he made his way to his feet, rubbing his injured leg. "Well if you two could go up on deck and check the robots, I will go down to see the Professor and ask him to look at my leg. Once we are finished, I will come up and see you all."

The twins headed for the stairs while Tobias hobbled down to the Professor's room. Walking around the circle, he stopped just behind one of the ghostly figures. It was translucent and he could see Sabella through its body. Curiosity getting the better of him, he reached out to touch the strange figure, but before he could electricity jumped out and connected with his fingers making him reel back in pain and rub his burnt hand. Thinking it was not the best idea to meddle he continued to the Professor's quarters. Knocking on the door he walked straight in. "Professor," he called.

"Please come in," the Professor squeaked.

Before Tobias could even close the door, the Professor started gibbering and mumbling, his voice getting higher and higher as he tried to make excuses and justify himself.

"Please, Professor, may I at least sit down," said Tobias.

"My leg is hurting, anyway I am not here to question you, I simply need to start piecing together this jigsaw puzzle. I am hoping to find some answers. So firstly, where did the Compton come from?"

Sheepishly, the Professor looked at him, "I built it; it was me."

Slamming his fist onto the desk making the Professor jump and nearly fall from his chair, Tobias shouted, "I will not ask you again, do not take me for a fool."

"Please calm down, Captain, let me explain," Professor Brumbles said shaking at Tobias' actions.

"I am still waiting," uttered Tobias.

Nervously, fearing the wrath from Tobias, the Professor began to explain.

"Honestly, please believe me when I say I did build the Compton, it is all my own work. From the automatic sails to the sunlight beam, they were all invented by me. Now the inside of the Compton unfortunately, I didn't build it."

"So where did it come from?" asked Tobias who was trying to calm down after getting some answers.

"I found it."

"What do you mean you found it? It couldn't have just been lying around," replied Tobias his voice rising once more.

"Captain, please," begged the Professor, his hands nervously shaking. "I did find it. Twenty miles east of Castle Cove there is a place called Steep Hill Cove. Once every hundred years the tide goes out further than any other time, the result is that the water is completely drained from the cove. It was on this day that I walked across the island looking for ingredients to do an experiment. When I looked over the top of the cliff into the cove there it was, just sat there on the rocks."

"What was?" Tobias asked.

"The ship was, Captain. Well, actually not a ship but more of a submarine shaped vessel. It was black with no windows or doors, but there was a hatch. Well, once I had raised it from the bottom the hatch was opened," said the Professor nervously.

"What did you find?" Tobias asked.

"Nothing but what you see here. The pillared corridor, the rooms and the engine. I just thought it was an old shipwreck of some sort. The engine was in good condition, strangely it was also running. So once raised I built the Compton around it. I never thought for one minute it would be so important. I'm so sorry, Captain."

"Hmm," mumbled Tobias as he leaned forward and stroked his beard. "Maybe it was a good thing you did find it. It could have been lost forever. Tell me was there anybody on it, or any signs of inhabitants?"

"No, Captain, it was exactly the same as what you see here. But I do believe there are many other corridors and rooms yet to be discovered. I don't seem to have the power to get into them."

"What makes you say that?" asked Tobias.

"It's simply massive, Captain, a lot bigger than the areas we occupy aboard it," the Professor explained. "Just look at the Compton itself, I built that around it like a second skin. I can show you."

"Yes, I would like to see it," Tobias nodded.

"Then please follow me, Captain," said the Professor.

Walking from his quarters, they walked around Sabella, the ghosts and up onto the deck. Opening the door, they stepped out into the cold, crisp air.

Going to the port side, past the twins and Jester, who were still cleaning arrows from the deck, the Professor took a strange key from his pocket. Bending down he placed it into a slot in one of the deck plates and turned. There was a loud clunk and a hatch opened up. Looking down, Tobias could see a metal ladder disappearing down into the darkness.

"After you please, Captain," pointed the Professor.

Stepping onto the first rung very gingerly with his bad leg still hurting he descended into the darkness. As he climbed down the ladder he looked around. He was now in a void about two meters wide which separated the two vessels. Everything was eerily lit by purple neon's which stretched the whole length of the ship in either direction. Stepping off the ladder onto a platform he waited for the Professor to join him. Looking around he could see the Compton's super structure, the big nuts and bolts sticking out which held together the steel plates. Looking down he followed the edges until they disappeared into darkness deep below. He could hear ice breaking at the bow. It made a scraping sound as large chunks rubbed down the side of the ship.

Eventually, he was joined by the Professor. "Right, Captain, I will now explain, as you can see you are standing between the

Compton which I built and the strange vessel here," he said pointing to his left, "As I mentioned it's as big as the ship as I made the super structure to fit around it. You can also see it's shaped like a giant fish, flat in the body with fins at the side, which makes me think it's an underwater craft. There are no physical signs of doors or windows, the only way in is where we have just entered. The engine was functional when I found it but there are no signs on how the craft propels itself. I have adapted it with the aid of large magnets to propel the ship along. It doesn't need fuel, as you saw in the engine room it is fuelled by a strange fluid which are self-regenerating. Then you have the outer skin itself, it is not any metal that I have ever seen or found. It can't be drilled, doesn't dent, you can't even scratch the surface. It's an incredible substance a marvellous piece of engineering."

"That it is," grumbled Tobias. "One that you took credit for. I just wish you had told us when you had found it. It may hold the key to many unanswered questions. One thing I am sure of is that you have found something that doesn't belong here. I am certain by what happened to Sabella means in some way it's connected to her and her people."

"So what happens now?" asked the Professor quietly.

"Absolutely nothing. There are a thousand and one questions to be answered but until Sabella wakes up if she wakes up, they will have to be left unanswered. All we can do is get her home safely to Castle Cove, as soon as we are in range, we need to contact Marmaduke informing him of the events that have happened. You never know, Professor, you may have just found the answer to protecting the orbs from Mortigan, but by not telling us about your find earlier you may also have caused his escape and set the wheels in motion for all-out war between good and evil."

Chapter 24

The Compton had made good time across the ocean in very favourable weather. Tobias had decided to leave the sunlight beam permanently on through day and night, as now they knew that the evolved breed of warrior could move within the shadows of the sun.

There had been no incidents or attacks, in fact it had been eerily quiet, even in the dead of night which worried Tobias in some ways. Did this mean that Mortigan was planning something much more spectacular than just attacking the Compton? Was he biding his time in some forgotten deep part of the ocean, planning his assault on acquiring all the orbs, and ultimately completing domination?

With sails up the ship glided along in warm, sunny weather. Standing on the bow Tobias peered across the calm blue sea. He had checked on Sabella as the others also had, every day, stopping for brief moments to look at her suspended in a ball of electricity. In case she could hear him, he would always speak to her, tell jokes, or just plainly gabble on about everyday happenings on the ship.

One day he stood there chatting as usual when right before his eyes something dropped to the ground. Looking down he could see the remains of the arrow which had been embedded in her chest. It was the first sign that just maybe she was on the road to recovery and that the ghosts stood in the circle around her were healing her, slowly bringing her back to health. In his excitement he called the rest of the crew down to see the black poisoned bit of metal that now lay on the floor, none were happier than Jester who had loyally kept up his daily duties of tidying, dusting and polishing her quarters. He even took from the shelf the book she had been reading the day they left for the mountain, carefully placing it on the desk opening it up to the exact page she had been reading from.

Tobias gave Marmaduke regular updates on Sabella's health, who himself was very worried about her as he couldn't see what was happening. It was a lot worse for him being at the castle hearing stories of ghosts and Sabella floating in a huge ball of electricity. At least he had a way of communicating with the ship. Every day without fail he would project himself into Sabella's training room for his daily reports. Tobias would then leave and take up his normal position stood at the bow where he would spend hours just staring out to sea.

It was on one particular day that Tobias shut the door to Sabella's quarters to head up on deck. They were close to home now everyone was excited about seeing Castle Cove.

Jester was just finishing up his daily routine when he heard the door go. Thinking it was the captain coming back in he carried on with what he was doing.

"Hello, Jester, is there any food around? I'm starving," said a familiar voice.

The little robot span around so quickly he nearly toppled over. "Sabella it's you, you're better, you're alive."

"Of course, I am," Sabella laughed. "Why wouldn't I be? I feel great although I can't remember much now, it's very odd that I woke up in the middle of the pillared corridor, also where is Tobias and the twins?" Sabella asked looking at Jester whose big round eye was blinking with excitement.

"The captain is up on deck, Miss Sabella, I think he ought to explain all that's been going on. How about some food?" Jester enquired trying to stop her asking him any more questions.

"I would love something," she answered back. "It doesn't feel like I have eaten for weeks, I don't think I have ever been so hungry."

"So what will it be?" Jester asked as he opened the flap in his belly and produced a nugget. Taking it out, he placed it into the palm of her hands.

Closing her eyes, Sabella thought about fish and chips. When she opened her eyes again, she looked at the feast before her. "That is the best food I have ever smelt." She grinned, sitting on the end of her bed and tucking straight in. It took a final helping of apple pie and cream, followed by a large chunk of chocolate cake before she felt full. Reaching up, she stroked her brow and squinted.

"Are you alright, Miss Sabella?" Jester asked.

"Yes, my little friend, I'm fine, I just have images flashing in my head like being badly injured and strange looking people around me."

"You need to go and see Tobias; he will give you some answers," Jester said, so happy to see his master again.

"Maybe I will go see him then I shall come back down for a soak in the bath." Sabella talking as if no time had passed at all.

"As always, I will have it ready for you, Miss Sabella," said Jester eager to please.

"Thank you, Jester," Sabella said patting him on the head, making her way to the door; she stepped out into the pillared corridor.

All was back to normal, gone was the circle, ghosts and the walls had closed back in leaving no sign of what was there only a few hours ago. Walking up the stairs she went through the door at the top and was instantly taken back by how warm it was. There was no chill in the air, no ice on the deck, no views across a barren white landscape. Instead she looked out over a lovely blue sea with the sun high in the sky and a gentle warm breeze which blew through the sails. It was all so confusing. It was like a part of the journey home was missing. Glancing up towards the wheelhouse she waved at Paiter who frantically waved back. Putting her finger up to her mouth she signalled to him to be quiet as she wanted to sneak up on Tobias.

Leaning around the corner she could see the captain still stood at the bow looking out to sea. Slowly, she crept up the deck and stood right behind him. "Captain," Sabella shouted making him jump at least a foot in the air.

Spinning around he grabbed hold of her and lifted her up. "You're alright," Tobias grinned before apologising for his sudden outburst of emotion.

"Tobias what is going on?" Sabella asked. "Firstly, I wake up in the corridor, then everyone is extremely happy to see me. To really confuse me the weather is warm and sunny. Can you please tell me what is happening? Has something occurred that I have missed out on?"

"Well you didn't exactly miss out," Tobias explained. "You made it happen."

"I have no idea what you are talking about," Sabella replied. "I can't remember a thing."

"OK well what I'm about to tell you came as a shock to us all. At what point do you remember up to?" Tobias asked.

Holding her head in her hands she racked her brains. "Well I remember the trip to the mountain, the bomb, fighting the warriors and something about the island sinking, I think you hurt your leg. I also remember Mortigan was here near the ship but after that it all goes a bit hazy."

"Well you must remember you told me you had doubts and concerns about the Professor? You said you didn't think he would be able to build the engine room and parts of the ship," said Tobias.

"Yes, I do recall that," Sabella said.

"Well you were right to think like that. The ship is in fact two ships, one inside the other. All you can see is what the Professor built but what you can't see is the inner ship. It's something to do with you, Sabella."

"I don't understand," she said confused.

"Let me try to explain. We were fighting the warriors and losing, you were having a battle with Mortigan who was about to attack the ship. At the same time, the Professor got the sunlight beam working. In all the commotion on deck you got injured."

"Keep going," Sabella prompted.

"Well your injuries were so bad we thought you were dead at one point. I carried you downstairs, but as I reached the corridor things started happening. The ship or more to the point the inner ship came to life. The pillars started flashing, parts of the walls then started to move back to form a circle. Then the most bizarre thing of all happened. Four ghostly figures rose from the floor before gliding across to me and looking down at you. Taking you from me they encased you in a ball of electricity; there you stayed until now."

"I think I understand it; that explains some of the images I have been having of four ghostly figures. It also makes sense why the sun is now shining and it's so warm. I can't believe I have been incapacitated for so long, no wonder I feel so good. Do we know any more about the ship?" Sabella asked.

"Not really," Tobias replied.

"I was hoping now that you are well, you can start looking into it as I'm sure it's from your civilization. The best place to start is by talking with the Professor. He can fill you in on all that he knows."

"I may do that straightaway. How far away are we from Castle Cove?" Sabella asked.

"Only a day now," Tobias replied, "We should see land by day break tomorrow."

"One last question although I think I already know the answer. Mortigan is free, isn't he?"

"Yes," nodded Tobias, "No matter what happened on Stenbury, he would have escaped. In the end Sabella we were too late. At least now we know Mortigan has escaped, we can prepare. The worst thing would have been if he had surprised us but at least now we can be ready."

"I need to start searching about how I'm linked to it all, including the Compton. I have also lost valuable study and training time. With Mortigan now free I need all the help I can get. I'm looking forward to getting back to Castle Cove with Marmaduke and I being able to start the next stage of my training. I'm off to see the Professor now so I will talk to you later, Tobias."

"It's so good to have you back with us Sabella, I thought we had lost you."

"It's good to be back," Sabella replied, "Besides I can't go anywhere, who would be here to make your life difficult if I wasn't around?"

Laughing, she left Tobias looking out to sea; at least now he had a smile on his face as she headed down to see the Professor. Walking along the pillared corridor Sabella paused and looked around. Where was she even going to start to piece together all of this? If a wise old head like Marmaduke who had trained future sorcerers for hundreds of years had no answer, then she had a big challenge on her hands and it was going to be far from easy.

Walking along she stopped at the Professor's room and knocked. She could hear footsteps quickly moving about the floor as the door opened.

"Sabella," Professor Brumbles squealed in excitement. "Please come in."

"Thank you, Professor," Sabella replied stepping through the doorway.

"I can't believe it's you. You look so well, please sit down," he added ushering her to a chair.

She looked across the room and saw the twins who were both flat out on their backs and rigged up to monitors with wavy lines and blips moving across the screens. Wires and circuitry stuck out from their arms and legs.

"What are the twins doing here?" Sabella asked. "Are they alright?"

"They are fine," explained the Professor. "Just some follow on work from what they sustained after the last battle. They had a lot of damage trying to protect the Compton, it's taken me a week to get them back to health, but they are fine now so please don't worry."

"The thing is, Professor, I do worry about them, they are so brave and courageous, sometimes it borders on being a bit foolhardy but the more time I spend with them the more I realise that they would die for me, that makes me both so very grateful and sad. I know now that I couldn't go anywhere without them by my side," said Sabella.

"They are very loyal, Sabella; they would protect you with their lives. They will always get injured and I will always have to fix and repair them but that's who they are. It is not the twins you have come to see me about is it?" the Professor asked sitting down at his desk.

"No, Professor, it's not. I have spoken to Tobias who has told me some things, but not everything. He has suggested that I come and talk with you." Sabella had so many questions that needed answering.

"I am very sorry, Sabella, I didn't know the ship belonged to you. I only found it, please believe me," he gabbled, getting all frustrated and agitated.

"Calm down, Professor," she said reassuring him. "What's done is done, it's in the past. Mortigan is free, that we do know. If we can find out what kind of craft we are sitting in, then it may help us destroy him. So why don't you start from the beginning. I won't ask any questions I promise I will just sit and listen."

So began hours of talking in which the Professor explained how he found the strange looking ship, through to building the Compton around it and finally seeing what happened when Tobias brought her down the stairs after being injured. They then went up on deck so Sabella could see for herself the strange looking craft. Eventually, she did get to sit down and eat dinner with Tobias where they asked a lot more questions, digging themselves a deeper and deeper hole into the strange mystery of the weird looking ship that they now travelled in.

With time getting late Sabella headed back to her quarters, leaving Tobias to prepare things for their arrival in the morning. Stepping through her door she looked around. What were all these strange symbols and shapes? She was desperate for answers but with so many years of fact and non-fact, was the truth now so far adrift and lost in years of storytelling that she may never find the answers. Maybe the old books held a small clue.

Sitting at her desk she began a night-long reading session in her search to find answers.

Chapter 25

"Morning, Miss Sabella," came a familiar voice as a big round eye peered up at her.

Lifting her head off the desk she stretched and yawned.

"Morning Jester, it's good to see your face smiling back at me in the morning. What time is it?" asked Sabella.

"Ten o'clock, Miss Sabella," the robot told her.

"Ten," she shouted. "Oh no, I'm late for Marmaduke," she said jumping up closing the book she had been reading.

"Please don't panic I have already informed sir that you worked late last night and shouldn't be disturbed. I have also explained that you will see him once the ship has docked. The captain has also called on you and asked me to wake you, as soon we will be seeing land. I have run you a bath and put out clean clothes. Is there anything else you need me to do before I leave you and help prepare the ship for docking?" asked Jester.

"No thanks, Jester. I don't know what I would do without you. I will see you before we dock."

The little robot headed off leaving her to enjoy a quick bath before getting dressed and heading up on deck. Stepping out of the door she breathed deeply putting her face to the sun, enjoying its warmth on her skin.

"I can see land," shouted Keltal.

"Over there," pointed Kaylum.

Walking up towards Tobias, she looked up as the huge sails were retracted. The Compton slowed down to a crawl powered solely by her own engine. Reaching the bow, she stood next to the captain, "Good morning."

"Morning," Tobias joked. "It's nearly the afternoon," he said trying not to laugh.

"It's not funny, I was up late last night reading, trying to get my head around all this confusion," yawned Sabella.

"Did you have any luck?" Tobias asked.

"Not really, I seem to be going 'round in one big circle." Sabella sounding frustrated.

"I'm sure once you can find a starting point it will all start falling into place. There's got to be something out there, all information can't just have vanished," Tobias said trying to reassure her.

The twins came up and joined them. "I can never thank you two enough for what you have done. You have given me great belief that whatever Mortigan throws at us we can match him. So thank you from the bottom of my heart."

"We are right by your side, Sabella," said Kaylum.

"Always," added Keltal.

"There it is," shouted Tobias. "We are home."

As they all looked, they could see the beautiful stone castle coming into view, nestling in the turquoise blue cove, its towers standing high over the outer walls with flags slowly being raised up the poles, signifying their homecoming. Although tinged with sadness at Mortigan's escape and the failing of the mission, it was so good to be back home. Sabella also knew she was a step closer to her mother, her fate and of course the fire orb.

Slowly, Paiter expertly brought the Compton to rest against the giant stone sea wall. The bow and stern lines were attached before the engine was shut down. The ship now gently rocked back and forward in the tide looking magnificent against the backdrop of the castle.

Keltal and Kaylum lifted the gangplank into position before they took their place in the line-up of the crew to see the captain and Sabella safely off the ship.

It still felt strange for Sabella seeing the wall complete and not in five pieces like she remembered it. Stepping off the gangplank before giving a final wave to her loyal crew they walked towards the steps. Pausing at the top she looked at Tobias.

"I'm scared of what I will find on the other side," she sighed.

"Well that makes two of us. Try and put it out of your mind for a little while longer, let's go to the castle and see Marmaduke. We really need to tell him about the trip also Mortigan's escape. We definitely need to warn him about the warriors being able to walk in daylight. Anyway I'm hoping he will give us some clues on what we can expect when we step through the door to the other side. A few more hours really aren't going to make that much difference to the outcome."

"I suppose not," Sabella answered sadly.

Walking down the stairs they headed across the sand to the gates.

"Open them up," a voice shouted.

There was a familiar loud clunk and the big iron gates started to open.

"Now remember Sabella, look happy. You are their protector they know nothing of what is happening or what might happen in the future."

"It still feels strange not being honest with them. It feels like I'm a fake, I am failing them in some way."

"In some ways you are but there is no need to alarm them. They wouldn't understand the bigger picture for they know not of the orbs or the power they control. This planet was only a hiding place for them hidden among the many other planets for safekeeping away from the evil one. Unfortunately, by ways we don't know, Mortigan is out there somewhere. I don't think these people would understand if they knew. Now you need to greet your people and smile," said Tobias.

Walking forward under the arch they were met by thousands of cheering people. From within the crowd children came running out, handing Sabella gifts and flowers. Eventually, they did reach the steps, on getting to the top she turned and waved before heading to the safety of the castle. Stepping inside, the door shut with a bang, the outside noise and bright sunshine was gone. At last calm and tranquillity were the only sound coming from the gentle trickling of water running down the pillars.

Slowly, walking down the corridor she entered the grand room with the map of the sea in the floor, and one of the skies in the ceiling. No matter how many times she looked at it, it was still an amazing sight. From the top of the stairs came a very familiar voice.

"Welcome home," Marmaduke bellowed loudly before floating down towards them gently landing in front of them.

"I am sorry I wasn't outside to meet you, but as you will understand I had to see you from a distance, in order to make sure it was you and no one else."

"I understand," Sabella replied. "After all it was you yourself who told me not to trust anyone."

"I am most glad you have listened to me," Marmaduke replied with a small smirk on his face. "Anyway, I am relieved to have you home safely, you too, Tobias."

"Thank you, master," Tobias replied.

"But I sense it's not here you really want to be, is it Sabella?" asked the wise old man.

"Is it the fate of your mother and the fire orb you seek?"

"I need to know my mother is safe," Sabella's voice tinged with sadness.

"Well in that case you must go, but please understand me Sabella there is a real chance your mother has been slain by the chameleon warrior. You must prepare yourself for the worst. I know it's very hard for you, but we need you to focus on the fire orb, as your first encounter will be with the warrior himself," answered Marmaduke.

"Why do you say that?" Sabella asked.

"That ghastly creature has the orb; there is no question about that. I also know that the only way it can gain access back to here is through the portal doorway, which only opens when you pass through it," Marmaduke explained.

"What should I do?" Sabella asked.

Stroking his long white beard, the old man leaned forward. "Destroy it. The moment you step into the doorway, it too will try and cross over. Stay in the portal, do not leave it or you will lose your powers. At that very point you need to grab the warrior and kill it. But, Sabella, you must not drop the orb for although it will be in its box, it is still very fragile, breaking it would spell disaster. You have only a split second to act I'm afraid to say there is no room for error. If, or what I mean is when you have accomplished that, then you will know the fate of your mother. This is something sadly you have to do alone Sabella as we cannot help you in any way. I can't stress enough you only have one chance to get it right. It is as important as life, and death. Tobias will stay here, as I need to be advised on the peculiar happenings, and powers of the ship I have heard so much about. He will follow you through once we know the orb is safe."

"How will you know?" Sabella asked.

"Darkness Sabella, if you drop the orb then darkness will descend on us all."

"And what of Mortigan?" Sabella enquired. "Where is he?"

Marmaduke sighed. "Evil itself will be planning his next move, hoping the chameleon warrior returns bringing him the fire orb. It is a very powerful orb if he takes control of it, he will have control over the army of fire. More than likely at this time he will be hiding somewhere close by," Tobias said pointing to a dark, deep-sea trench on the map.

"The Professor has something he is inventing which may help locate him. Until we do, we must carry on as normal, so please accomplish your mission when you have done what you need to do, then please you must come back to us. The orbs are in danger and need to be found Sabella, we are running out of time," said Marmaduke.

Walking over to a pillar, Marmaduke touched a panel as a door in the wall opened.

"This secret passageway will take you to the beach. From here on in is a race between good and evil one that we must win. The element orbs are not safe, you must retrieve the fire orb and bring it back. Take care Sabella; remember don't be fooled by what you see."

"Just one last thing," Sabella asked, "How do I open the door?"

"The door is always open, Sabella, you just have to walk through it. Remember what I said to you, you are more powerful than you realise. The secret to opening the door is in your mind, you just need to believe it."

Chapter 26

Climbing down a rickety ladder Sabella walked along a dark and damp narrow tunnel, she bent down on her hands and knees, crawling out through a very tiny hole at the side of the castle wall. Shielding her eyes against the bright sun she quickly crossed the beach and stood next to the small stone staircase. Looking up at the top she slowly started to climb, her heart pounding against her chest in anticipation. Reaching the second to last step she paused. Everything that would happen in the future all hinged on what happened next.

Looking back at the beautiful castle with its flags flying high from each corner she felt sick with fear. She had to get it right. Taking one last deep breath and stepping up onto the last step she turned and faced out to sea. Closing her eyes, she bowed her head and stepped forward onto the wall.

In the blink of an eye the sun had turned to torrential rain. The angry clouds rolled across the sky accompanied by rumbles of thunder and flashes of lightning. The sea boiled and bubbled around her. As she stood on one of the five old pieces of wall holding a small wooden chest in one hand and a snarling angry chameleon warrior tightly around the neck in the other, she remembered what Marmaduke had told her. She had to stay halfway in the portal, keeping it open, retaining her powers as for some strange reason not known to her or anyone else, she would lose them the minute the portal was shut. That's why her mother had long since lost hers.

Turning her head, she faced the chameleon warrior which was flailing its arms around and snapping its teeth. It then gave her the ultimate test of willpower by changing itself from an ugly looking creature to her sister Ashley. It even manipulated its voice to sound like her. The devilish beast pleaded with her time and time again to be freed from her vice like grip, but Sabella stayed strong and held her nerve.

Playing its final card, it turned once more from her sister to her mother, again pleading for mercy. Tears welled up in Sabella's eyes as she looked at the pain she was inflicting on what appeared to be her mother.

"Stay strong," she whispered to herself, "Don't trust your eyes."

With that she slowly closed them and looked into the heart of the warrior, but there wasn't one, just a cold dark mass of pure killing machine. With anger building inside she opened her eyes staring at the warrior for one last time. It had converted back to its ugly self, hissing and snarling once more as it realised it was about to die.

Squeezing her hand together the chameleon burst into flames before slipping through her hands, ending up a pile of ash on the floor before the next gust of wind picked it up and swept it out to sea.

Laying the chest down, she stepped out of the portal and slumped beside it. Her energy levels greatly diminished now, she had lost her powers. Looking up she stared along the five pieces of broken wall being pounded by the waves. Glancing across at the stony beach which led to a grassy bank, wild flowers grew where once a castle stood.

Slowly, getting to her feet she picked up the chest which felt a lot heavier than before. Struggling she made her way down step by step, nearly slipping a few times on the seaweed as she went. At the bottom she placed the chest down on the sand as she just couldn't lift it anymore. It would take ages to get it back to the house, she just didn't have the strength to lift it let alone fight against the gale force wind. The needle like sea spray was hitting her in the face along with the lashing rain.

She was desperate to know the fate of her mother but she couldn't leave the chest containing the orb of fire alone on the beach. Bending down she put all her energy into lifting the box up one last time but it just slipped through her hands.

"I will take that for you," came a familiar voice.

Looking up Sabella was greeted by a big round grinning face, "Tobias," she shouted over the wind, "I did it, I killed the warrior, but I have lost my strength and can't carry the chest."

Putting his hand on her shoulder he leaned forward. "Don't worry, I will bring the orb. It is safe now. You have done your part in this; now go to your mother."

Giving him a half-smile, she turned and took off across the beach, faster than her legs could carry her to the house. Climbing the small steps cut into the bank she battled the wind and the rain to reach the front door. Eventually, she fell into the porch out of the storm. On her knees, she reached out to grab the door handle but there wasn't one. In fact there was no door; it was completely blocked up.

Standing up she stuck her head out from the porch and was surprised to see the windows had too disappeared. Every opening in the house had gone; it had turned into some kind of sky bunker. There appeared to be no way in, and no way out.

Standing in the porch she shouted at the top of her voice for her mother but there was no reply. Looking at the symbols around the door she noticed two she had never seen before, like handprints. On closer inspection they seemed quite small, about the same size as hers. Stretching out she placed her left hand in one side and her right hand in the other. A bright blue line appeared to trace each hand in turn. When it had finished a mechanical sound could be heard deep under the house.

Standing back from fear of what might happen she was amazed to see the doors and windows start to reappear before her very eyes. Within seconds the house was back to normal having retracted what appeared to be some sort of defence system. Rushing to the door she grabbed the handle and turned it. The door swung open slowly and she stepped in. It was eerily quiet with only the ticking of the old grandfather clock to be heard.

Standing in the hallway she peered first into the lounge then into the kitchen. Everything was neat and tidy there appeared to be no damage. Walking across the hall she looked down the hallway towards the library.

"Mum," Sabella called, "Mum, are you here?"

She could hear a key being turned in a lock and a latch being slid back. The library door then opened. Bosen came running out, his paws sliding on the floor as he tried to rush up the hallway towards her. Bending down she picked him up, hugging him tightly as he wriggled with excitement in her arms.

Then the face of her mother appeared slowly from behind the door. "Sabella, is that you?" Mrs Rose whispered.

"Mum, it is me," Sabella called out running down the hallway into her mother's arms.

Squeezing her tightly, sobbing with pure joy at the sight and sound of her mother, it was then that she winced in pain. Letting her go Sabella looked at her closely.

"You're hurt we need to get you help."

"I'm fine," Mrs Rose reassured her. "Thanks to Professor Billingham," not wanting to tell her daughter how close to death she had come at the hands of the warrior.

Then Mr Wolverton appeared from the library door. He was also limping quite badly.

"Is someone going to tell me what happened here?" Sabella asked.

"All in good time, Sabella," replied her mother, "Just tell us one thing. Is it dead?"

"Yes, it's dead," Sabella replied, as they all let out a sigh of relief.

"And what of the orb?" asked Mr Wolverton.

"That's safe too Tobias, or should I say Mr Brookes is bringing it up to the house. So now are you going to tell me what's happened?" Sabella asked.

"Not right now, you have so many questions that need answering, as do I and Mr Wolverton. Please let's start dealing with them tomorrow. A lot of things have changed since all of this began Sabella, and a lot of things are going to change in the future.

"Just for one day to celebrate your safe return let's be together and be grateful for that, for I have my daughter back I want to spend one last day with you as just that, my daughter. It would make me so happy," Mrs Rose said as tears welled up in her eyes, she hugged her tightly.

"It would make me happy too, Mum. I will always be Sabella your daughter. After all that has happened, it doesn't change a thing for me," she smiled. Not wanting to push for any more answers she then changed the subject.

"Now I take it you still have some cakes baked ready for my return?" Sabella giggled.

"No," replied her mother, "But I can soon bake some." A smile returning to her face.

Wrapping their arms around each other's shoulders they headed off towards the kitchen.

"See you tomorrow Sabella, it's good to have you home," called Mr Wolverton.

"Thank you," Sabella called back, "Don't forget, Tobias, he will be here soon."

Closing the kitchen door, Sabella and her mother spent the rest of the day and evening talking, laughing and of course baking lots of cakes. It was like old times with everything being back to normal, almost as if her recent journey in space and time had never happened. They both knew it had of course and that they would both have to approach some delicate subjects, such as her sister, father, the orbs, Castle Cove, her civilization and the strange powers she possessed.

With the sun setting Sabella felt very tired and gave a big yawn. Giving her mother a hug, she headed upstairs to bed. Walking across the landing she stopped at her sister's room and pushed the door open. She felt so sad, not because of losing her sister. The thing that had impersonated her sister all her life was a chameleon warrior. She was sad she never actually got to meet her at all. Unfortunately, she had been killed many years ago when she was just a baby.

Shutting the door once more she walked along to her room. Looking around she smiled to herself at how young and girly it all looked with pink bed covers, with her big fluffy slippers tucked under the end. It was truly a world away from her life now. In a matter of weeks, she had gone from Sabella the girl who lived a normal life with no cares in the world to being Sabella the girl who had not only the world, but the universe on her shoulders. She had become the protector of all the element orbs and the only one who could keep good and evil side by side.

Walking across the room she peered out into the gloom. The rain and wind had died down, there was a strange orange glow across the sky. Some of Tobias' weird looking cows were grazing on the grass which over looked the cove. Pulling the curtains shut, she walked over and sat on the bed. Putting on the bedside light she was soon joined by Bosen who curled up beside her and was soon fast asleep.

Tucking herself under her cover she picked up her favourite book called 'My Iron Island'. She could only manage a couple of lines as understandably her mind was elsewhere.

Climbing out of bed, she walked over to the window and opened it. Drawn to the night sky she looked up through the gaps in the clouds. Thousands of little specs of light shone brightly back at her against the black abyss of space. Hidden up there amongst the hundreds of thousands of stars was Knighton, lost in a distant part of space, maybe thousands or millions of light years away. Anyway wherever it was, no one on Earth had the technology to see or travel that far. People would never believe, or rather didn't want to believe that there could be other inhabited planets out there in the clear starry night sky. Humans had travelled into space and gone to the moon but in terms of space travel they had gone just a millimetre. Earth was no threat to anyone, just a tiny blue planet floating in the middle of deep space. But it was now under threat, and who's to say that time travellers from different planets and galaxies were not walking amongst us on Earth.

Everything had now changed for her. Sabella now knew that things and life existed outside the comfort zone of Earth, something bigger than anyone could comprehend. A war was raging across space and time as it had done for millenniums. A war between good and evil, a battle of the element orbs.